# WALL

A STEEL BONES MOTORCYCLE CLUB ROMANCE

CATE C. WELLS

Cover art and design by Clarise Tan of CT Cover Creations.
Editing by Nevada Martinez.
Proofreading by Raw Book Editing http://www.rawbookediting.com

Special thanks to Jean McConnell of The Word Forager, Erin D., Sarah L., and always, Louisa.

❀ Created with Vellum

# PROLOGUE

"Y ou sure you won't come, babe?" John's at the front door, helmet in hand, letting out the air conditioning.

My head's pounding. I've been grinding my teeth at night, and the dull ache only gets worse as the day wears on. Aspirin won't touch it anymore.

"Nah. I've got a headache."

He puts his helmet down on the entry table. I wish he'd shut the door. The afternoon sun is unbearably bright.

He clumps to the bathroom and rummages around in the medicine cabinet, drops something, and curses.

I tuck myself as far as possible into the corner of the sofa and draw an afghan up to my nose.

"What are you looking for?" Now I can hear him pawing underneath the sink.

"Aspirin."

"On the kitchen counter." I channel surf, looking for something to put me to sleep. There's a home improvement show with a man who looks like my father-in-law. He's talking about chimney pots. Perfect.

John lumbers past the TV, and then he squats by the sofa. He goes to smooth my hair, and I duck. It's really greasy. I haven't shampooed it in...a while.

"Here." He holds out two white pills in his giant palm. My husband's a big man. Remember that show from the 80s where a sasquatch lived with a family in the suburbs? In any given social situation, John's that bigfoot. He's not hairy, though. He's a good-looking guy. Rugged. The lumberjack type.

I push his palm away. "It won't help."

He sighs. "You're dehydrated."

"I just need some rest."

"You got up at eleven."

"I was up late last night." I wish he'd stop arguing with me. We both know he'll have a better time without me. I'm crappy company these days. "You're gonna be late for the run."

"Maybe I shouldn't go. If you're not feelin' good." He eyes the door. Which is still wide open.

"No. You go. I'm just gonna take a nap."

"I could take a nap with you." He tries to give me a grin, but worry crinkles the corners of his eyes. He looks tired and worn down, too. He needs a day with the boys. There's no reason we both need to be miserable.

"Baby, I want you to go."

He stays beside me for a moment longer, searching my eyes. I make a show of yawning, and I turn my head. He loves riding his bike. He'll have a great time. Maybe while he's gone, I can drag my butt into the shower. I could make a roast. I'd need to get up now to defrost it.

Maybe I could make pasta.

John rises to his feet. "Are you sure, baby?"

I wave my hand, rolling over to face the back of the sofa,

tugging the afghan tighter around my body. Eventually, he tromps out, thankfully shutting the door behind him.

JOHN'S LATE. I check my phone for the hundredth time. No text. He always texts when he's gonna be late. He's a firefighter, so he could've been called in. It's happened before. But he calls or texts when he gets called in.

I pace the living room. It's four o'clock in the morning. The run should have ended hours ago. Smoke and Steel is a club for firefighters and EMTs. They party, but most of them have babysitters they need to relieve.

I should call again. But if his voicemail picks up immediately one more time, I'm going to tear my hair out.

What if there was an accident and his phone is on the side of the road, shattered? What if he's in an ambulance, and they don't know he's allergic to penicillin?

I'm being crazy. He'll walk in any minute with a perfectly reasonable explanation, and I'll look like I've lost my damn mind. I glance down. Am I wearing the same clothes as yesterday? No, it's been longer. Maybe I've had these on since Friday? Crap. I was off on Friday. These are the sweats I put on when I came home from work Thursday night. I crane my neck and take a sniff. Not good.

I should take that shower. When was the last time I washed my hair? Maybe Wednesday before work?

But what if John calls while I'm in there?

Or what if the hospital calls, and I have to leave? Crap, I can't go looking like this. I've totally let myself go. I'd put more effort in if I didn't have to wear scrubs every day. If I had an office job, I'd do more than a messy bun.

I hear a vehicle turn down our cul de sac. I freeze. My

heart leaps into my throat. Is that a bike? No. A car. It keeps driving past our house. I stay there, my stomach sinking, motionless in the middle of my living room, and stare unseeingly around the two-story Colonial John and I bought three years ago.

My gaze catches on our wedding photo, hanging above the TV console. I'm barely nineteen, five foot three, and all smiles. John takes up most of the frame. He towers over me. He's not much of a smiler, but his eyes are twinkling like crazy. He's happy.

He hasn't looked like that in a while.

I lower my gaze to the rest of the living room. There are several half-empty Diet Coke cans on the coffee table. The carpet needs vacuuming. There's a pile of newspapers in my grandmother's rocking chair. I keep meaning to call and cancel the subscription.

Things haven't been going so well. Life has thrown us some curveballs lately.

But John and I are regrouping now. We're focusing on us.

Where *is* he?

Another vehicle turns down our street. This time, there's a crunch of asphalt and a sputter as his engine cut off.

He's home.

A wave of relief rocks me on my heels, followed immediately by a surge of fury. Where has he been? How dare he make me worry like this, on top of everything! He better have a damn good excuse.

I want to run outside, make sure with my own eyes that he's okay. But I'm also shaking with rage and fear.

It's an eternity before his feet crunch on the driveway. His big boots stomp up the walk and across the porch. His tread is lighter than usual, but if he's trying to be stealthy, he's failing. For some reason, he lingers at the door. Maybe he's looking for his keys.

Well, I'm not helping him out. I'm on the far side of the living room, arms crossed so hard I'm cutting off circulation to my hands.

He eases the door open. He probably thinks I'm asleep. He should know better. I spend most nights wide awake on the sofa now, watching old sitcoms like *I Love Lucy* and *The Carol Burnett Show* until I pass out sitting up. It's the only way I can sleep.

John ducks through the doorframe and stops when he sees me. His helmet's hanging from his hand, his cut's folded over his arm, and his black T-shirt's untucked. He looks like hell.

He clears his throat. "You're up."

The smell of whiskey hits me from all the way across the room. "Did you drive home drunk?"

He scrubs the back of his neck. "No. I been sober a few hours now."

"How drunk were you that you still smell like a distillery, and you've been sober for hours?" My voice is shrill, even to my own ears. I'm so pissed. He's a mess. His eyes are blood-shot, and his brown hair's sticking up at all angles, which is hard to accomplish with a crew cut.

"Very."

I sigh in exasperation. "Is that all you're gonna say?"

He's quiet for a long time. My anxiety ratchets even higher, sweat prickling the back of my knees. His expression is scaring me. I hardly recognize him. John's a stoic guy, a man of few words. I haven't seen this look on his face before.

He sinks down onto the couch. "Sit, will you?" He gestures to the ottoman facing him.

What's going on? What's happened?

"What's wrong? Oh, my God. Was there a bad fire? Is everyone okay?" My mind's running wild. There was a five-alarm a month or so ago, and a guy from John's station was hospitalized. An older couple didn't make it. John's been really torn up about it.

"No fire. Everyone's fine."

I should be relieved, but he's bent over, his forearms braced on his thighs, his head hanging. He looks defeated.

"Did you lose your job?"

"Can you sit, Mona?"

I do, my heart pounding quicker and quicker. Something's wrong. The room is so quiet. I can hear the blood rushing in my ears.

I want to smack him. Demand that he tells me what's going on. This is John, though. He does things in his own time. I bite my lower lip and force myself to wait.

The clock ticks on the wall. In the kitchen, the icemaker clatters.

John squares his shoulders, straightens his spine, and looks me in the eye. "Mona, I...I, uh. I've been with someone else."

I must have misheard. "What do you mean?"

"Last night...I, um. I was with someone else."

I press my hands to my face. Tears blur my eyes. My brain's stuck, but my body's tumbling forward without me.

"I don't understand."

"After the run. I got drunk. There was a woman. I, uh. I had sex with her."

Everything inside of me drops. Stomach. Heart. Like I didn't know it, but my whole self was held up by strings, and someone came along with a pair of scissors, and before I could blink—Snip. Snip. Crash.

I lurch to my feet. He stays there on the couch, still and rigid.

"No." Our wedding picture is on the wall. He changed the oil in my car yesterday before he left for the run. This doesn't make sense.

"Why?" I don't wait for him to answer. "Do you love her?"

"I don't really know her."

Is that better? Does that make it worse? I'm gonna puke. Oh, God. Acid sours my throat. "Who is she? Do *I* know her?"

"Her name's Stephanie. She hangs around the clubhouse."

I don't really know the people from the MC. John took me to a few events when he first joined, but the women were cliquey, and then recently, I don't really feel like going out much anymore.

I never worried, though. Steel and Smoke aren't a bunch of outlaw bikers or anything. They're family guys.

But there were women. Fun women who ride, who wear cowboy hats and painted-on jeans. Women who jump up to dance as soon as the music comes on.

Did I ever meet a Stephanie?

"What does she look like?" I stare down at my sweatpants. Not even yoga pants. Men's sweatpants with a cartoon Tasmanian devil on the thigh.

"I don't know—"

"You don't know?" My voice edges toward hysterical.

He doesn't answer. He hangs his head, and then a lifetime later, he lifts his chin and says, "I'm so sorry, Mona. I'm so fucking sorry."

"How many times?"

"I never done this before. I swear." He lets out a rattling breath. "God, Mona. I'm so sorry."

I don't recognize him. His face is shuttered, his red eyes are blank. I don't recognize this man at all.

I married John Wall. The best man I ever met. Tough. Kind. No bullcrap. He opens every door for me. Car doors. Restaurant doors. Our own front door. He saves lives. He mows my parents' lawn even though they've never tried to get to know him.

John Wall would *never* cheat on me.

"Why did you—?" My voice breaks halfway through.

I wait, and John stares over my shoulder, into the kitchen, that strange expression on his face, and the clock ticks and the fridge hums, until I can't take it anymore.

He doesn't have an answer. Or he doesn't know. Or he doesn't want to tell me it's because I'm disgusting. I've let myself go. I've fallen down, and I can't pull myself up by my bootstraps and make dinner for once or at least do something with my hair.

It's too much, and he's just sitting there. Like he's waiting to be dismissed. I run my tongue over my teeth. They're fuzzy. I have to go to work in two hours. And crap—my scrubs are still in the washing machine.

I can't do this.

"Get out."

It's a whisper at first. He flinches, and then he tentatively reaches out his hand in some reluctant, half-assed attempt to calm me down.

"Get out!"

My fists ball. "Get out! Get out! Get out!" I can't breathe; it sounds like I'm gasping for life.

"Mona." John rises to his full height, and he steps

forward, as if he can help, as if he's going to take care of me. This.

"Get out." I point, my arm shaking, all of me shaking.

He stands there for a long minute, that horrible empty look on his face, and then he walks out the door, shutting it softly behind himself.

## 1

MONA, 4 YEARS LATER

"Woo hoo!" Miss Janice's voice rings out as I pass her room. "Shift over?"

It is, almost. But I've always got a few minutes for my girl. I make sure Lorraine at the nurse's station doesn't seem to need anything, and I duck into Miss Janice's room. She's in her Geri chair. Must have been a good day.

"What are you up to, lady?" I drag the visitor's chair to a spot where it's not visible from the open door, and I plop down.

"Well, I had a bit of excitement today. Tommy visited!"

I heard about that. The cafeteria ladies were joking about how they'd better count the silverware.

"He bring your ring?"

Miss Janice's smile slips. "He forgot it again."

Bullcrap. That little punk only visits his grandmother when he's got a paper he needs her to sign. He's sold off her car, her deceased husband's truck, and boat. As far as I'm concerned, the sooner he bleeds her dry, and we're rid of him, the better. Her blood pressure's always sky high after he visits.

"I'm sure he'll remember next time." She's been asking him to bring her engagement ring from her house—that he now lives in—since she's been here. He's always got an excuse.

Miss Janice's frown melts away—she can't keep one long —and her cloudy blue eyes start twinkling. "Dr. Oldham came by while we were visiting."

"Did he?"

"He was looking poorly fed. He needs a good woman."

Dr. Oldham already has a good man at home, but I don't want to ruin Miss Janice's fun. "He's not my type."

"That man is everyone's type."

"Not mine. He's got a tragic flaw."

"Which is?"

"Vegetarian."

Miss Janice cracks up. "See? Poorly fed." Her laugh devolves into a hacking cough.

I freshen up her plastic cup with water from the sink. I need to have a word with the CNA about keeping her hydrated. Janice sips like a bird; she shouldn't be running out of water.

I keep up the conversation while she gets her cough under control. "Besides. I'm done with men. More trouble than they're worth."

She shakes her head. "You're much too young to say that. What are you? Twenty-five? Twenty-six?"

"Twenty-eight."

"See? Too young. There's a fella out there made perfectly for you. You'll see."

The usual, horrible feelings burble up inside me, and I stand quickly and make a show of getting myself a drink of water. I'm okay ninety-nine percent of the time. But then someone says something—and out of nowhere—I'm in a Looney Tunes cartoon and a safe crashes on top of my head.

John Wall sure did a number on me.

I catch a glimpse of myself in the mirror. I need to fix my face. I pinch my cheeks to get some color back. "I'm focusing on climbing the corporate ladder, you know that Miss Janice."

"You're much too sweet to be the big boss."

"That may be, but someone has to look out for you all."

It's criminal how some facilities are run. Shady Acres is one of the good ones, but the condition of the patients we get from some other places? It's a crying shame. Bed sores. Dehydration. You name it.

My ten-year plan is to get my RN and then my MBA. You can't change much in the trenches; you can only work yourself to the bone, which most of my colleagues do. You can only fix things if you have the right letters after your name.

I didn't used to have a fire lit under my butt. The year after John and I split near killed me, but one day, bawling in the shower, I just got sick of myself. I decided I needed to care about someone else for a while, and I took a good look around and realized I'm working with people who need me every day. And I could do more for them. So I dusted myself off, enrolled in a nursing program, and here I am.

I make my way back to the guest chair, grabbing two books on the way.

"You up to this?" I hold them up. "Sounds like you had a busy day. It was raining men."

"Hallelujah." Miss Janice snickers and holds her hand out. "Study group is in session. Now, where were we?"

I flip open the NCLEX-RN study guide and set it on her tray. It's way too heavy to lay in her hand.

"Bleeded and impaired hemostasis."

"Sounds interesting! Get my glasses."

I gently pluck them from the string around her neck and slide them on her nose.

"Thank you, my dear."

We spend the next fifteen minutes or so with Miss Janice quizzing me on the test to become a registered nurse. She was a lector at her church, so she has a lovely reading voice. When her voice starts cracking, I take the study guide and shelve it behind the collection of greeting cards from the folks in her congregation.

"You ready now?"

Miss Janice rests her head back, her eyelids beginning to droop. Reading takes a lot out of her. "Always. What are we on this evening?"

"Psalms, I believe."

A wistful smile softens the deep lines around her mouth. "My husband hated Psalms. Not enough action for him."

"More of an Exodus kind of guy?"

"Oh, yes. Daniel. Judges. Both Samuels. He was a boy at heart. He loved the stories." Her eyes get even dreamier, remembering.

I start to read, and she lets herself drift off. I keep going despites the snores. It's peaceful in the warmth, and fat snowflakes are starting to fall outside the window.

I don't notice so much when Janice is awake because she's so lucid and animated, but she's not doing so well. She's lost a lot of muscle mass lately. She's so tiny in her huge chair, mostly bifocals and a cloud of wispy white hair.

I read through another psalm until I figure she's passed out, and I shelve the Bible. Then I go on a hunt for the quilt she favors.

Sometimes I wonder if my parents will want me to fuss

over them when they're old enough for a place like Shady Acres. They've never had much use for me to this point, but a facility like this is a lonely place despite the constant bustle and noise.

I find the quilt on the top shelf in the wardrobe—how was she supposed to get it all the way up there?—and I lay it on her lap. Before I can sneak out, she rouses and reaches out for my hand.

I grab it and squeeze gently.

Her eyes are muzzy with sleep. "Lloyd?"

Lloyd was her husband. "He's not here, Miss Janice."

Tears well in her eyes. "I miss him."

I sit on the edge of her bed so we're face-to-face, and I grab her other hand. "I know."

My action draws her attention to her lap. "Where's my ring?"

My heart cracks. "It's at home. Your grandson's going to bring it."

She closes her eyes, and tears stream down her ruddy cheeks. "I never take my ring off. Where's Lloyd? Why am I here? I need my ring."

She pleads, gripping my hands with a strength I didn't think she had.

"This is Shady Acres Adult Living. I'm Mona. You're okay. It's going to be okay."

She so distraught, she's shaking. "I need my ring. Will you get it for me? I never take it off."

"Your grandson, Tommy, he says he'll bring it the next time he visits." I hate lying, and I hate that even with the sundowners, it's obvious that Janice knows I'm full of crap, too.

"No. *You* go get my ring. We're friends, aren't we?" She sounds so young, like a little girl wheedling her playmate.

I don't know what to say. "Of course, we're friends."

"Then, please go get my ring. I need it." She rubs her bare finger with her thumb. "It's an old mine-cut diamond with blue sapphires. Gold band. I left it on my bureau, in the jewelry box shaped like a piano. I didn't want anyone to steal it."

"I'm sure Tommy will bring it next time he comes."

Her sweet face becomes severe, and she clutches my hands even harder. There's an alertness to her now that had been absent. "You and I both know that boy is irresponsible. I need you to go and get it. *Please.*"

She reaches for a tissue, but she knocks the box onto the floor. I scoop it up and offer her one.

"You don't understand." She dabs at her eyes. "I don't have anything here that he gave me. He's been gone so long."

That barrage of awful feelings that I shook off earlier comes barreling back, full steam. It's such a nasty brew, bad memories and pain that does nothing but rot and fester, ignored but never gone. Never healed.

There's grief, first and foremost. Rage. Humiliation. Shame. Disappointment, although that word's nowhere near strong enough. And *missing*, the worst part of it all.

I *miss* the family I almost had.

And I miss John.

I told him to get out, and he did. Didn't even try to explain himself. I packed all his stuff, every last thing down to his half-used bar of Zest and the box of high school trophies in the attic. I put it on the front porch, he came and got it, and then he was gone.

He never argued, never begged me to take him back. I guess he took his out.

I miss him, though, and late at night or when I've had a

glass of wine too many, I wish I'd kept something. A shirt or a baseball cap. I could burn it in a bonfire. Make a fresh start.

Or so I could let myself be weak, just for a moment, and remind myself of how he smells.

Crap. Now I'm crying. I'm a weeper, always have been. I'm a sad crier, an angry crier, a sympathetic crier. I cry at movies, sunsets, songs on the radio. That's me. My parents were forever telling me to pull myself together. Never have been able to.

I help myself to a tissue. "Okay, Miss Janice. I'll get your ring for you."

"Promise." Her round, wrinkled face is fiercer than I've ever seen it.

"I promise."

"Number Five, Constantine Court. In the piano-shaped jewelry box on my bureau. There's a key under the ceramic frog in the flowerbed out front."

"I'll probably just ring the doorbell."

"All right. Suit yourself. And thank you, Cecily. You always were a good girl."

"You're welcome." I don't know who Cecily is, but if I get arrested rooting under a ceramic frog in Miss Janice's front lawn, that's the name I'm giving the police.

I say goodnight and head out for the evening. I think about dropping by Constantine Court and getting it out of the way, but the snow's picked up. I don't want to be out after dark. I drive home extra carefully; my car's not the best in bad weather.

When I get there, I'm stoked to see a kid shoveling my sidewalk. The local high school gives credit for community service.

I give the kid a wave as I pull into my drive. "Thanks!"

He looks old. Must be a senior.

Tomorrow, on my day off, I'll go on my fool's errand. Tonight, I'm going to curl up with my study guide and a hard seltzer. It's been a long week.

As I toe off my shoes and wander into the kitchen, I pull up my Friday night playlist on my phone. I blast country music from the 90s, my favorite, and then I turn on the TV in the family room. I can't stand being alone in a quiet house.

Lorraine, from work, thinks I should get a dog. I love dogs. We had a mutt named Gerard growing up, and until my parents noticed, he'd sleep in bed with me. He had the best terrible doggie breath.

A dog would be good company, but...I have bad dreams. I'd freak a dog out. And I'd never forgive myself if I kicked him coming out of a nightmare.

So, I think maybe it's better to stick with just myself. Keep busy. If I get bored, there's always something to do around the house.

It's enough.

## 2

### WALL

"Where you goin'?" Heavy pops his head out of his office and stops me on my way out the back. I'm zipping up my camo bibs. "You goin' huntin'?"

"Ain't no deer in those woods." The Steel Bones clubhouse abuts a hundred-acre parcel of undeveloped land, but there's too many dirt bikers, and it's too late in the season for bucks.

"What you doin' then?"

I shrug on my parka. "Deb says there's a stray dog."

"You gonna look for him?"

"Yup."

"Gimme a minute."

"I'll wait out back." I stomp down the hall toward the exit, making a ruckus. I'm a big man in hunting boots. I can't move no other way. I pat my pocket, making sure I remembered the baggie of kibble.

Outside, the sun's hiding behind a blanket of winter clouds. I draw in a deep breath. There's a bite and a dampness to the air. The storm they're callin' for is coming quicker than the weatherman said.

I glance around for a prospect. Mikey, the skinny one, is chopping wood for tonight's bonfire.

"Mikey!"

"Yeah, Wall?" He trots over.

I grab a grease pencil from my side pant pocket and tear a page from my little notepad. "In a few hours, or when there's two inches or so on the ground, head over to Shady Gap. Go here." I scrawl down an address. "Shovel the driveway and the walk. If the lady asks, say you're doin' community service. Don't wear your cut."

"Cool, man. Cool. I got you, man."

"Tomorrow morning, head over again. Six o'clock. Shovel again. Maybe lay down some salt tonight. Yeah." I dig in my pocket and peel a fifty off my roll. "Get the kind that's pet friendly. Keep the change."

"Thanks, man. Thanks. So, whose house this is?"

"It's my house."

"I thought you lived at the clubhouse."

"I do."

For a second, it looks like he's gonna pry, but he ain't that dumb. "Okay, man. I got you."

"Remember. No cut. You're in high school. You need community service hours."

He strokes his patchy beard defensively.

I stare him down.

"All right. If you say so, man. Got it."

The door slams, and Heavy tromps out in his bright orange puffy jacket.

I raise an eyebrow. "You seriously wearin' that?"

"You said we were looking for the dog, not hunting it. I don't wanna get shot doing a good deed."

I snort and head off toward the woods.

"So what kind of dog are we looking for?" Heavy has his phone out, dashin' off a text. The man is always working, always got a dozen irons in the fire. Still, he's decent company. He don't run off at the mouth, and he's one of the few men tall enough to keep up with my pace.

"Way Deb describes him, German Shepherd maybe."

"Where'd she see him?"

"She says he's been hangin' around the yard. Heads off to the woods as soon as he hears people comin'. She's been watchin' him from her office window."

"What's the plan?"

"I dunno." I scan the sky. Snow's gonna start any minute. Won't be able to look for tracks. "Guess we're lookin' for piles of dog shit."

Heavy guffaws. "Story of my life, man."

We set off in silence for the tree line, my eyes on the ground, Heavy's on his phone. I see more crushed beer cans than I'd like. When we get back, prospects are gonna have a chore.

About three years back, I got put in charge of facilities and prospects. Mostly by default. Heavy's more a C.E.O. now that Steel Bones Construction has taken off, and the other brothers with reliable sobriety and high school educations have other positions.

We pass Shirlene and Twitch's tree. She's got a folded lawn chair leanin' against it. Guess she's getting a little too old for sittin' on the ground, and Twitch ain't around to help her up no more. I shoot off a quick prayer. Twitch was a great man, gone too soon. When we come back, I need to remember to bring her chair in so it don't rust.

Once we're in the woods, the trees grow fairly far apart, so we cover a great deal of ground quickly. I don't see turds of any kind. Heavy ain't no help. Still got his nose in his phone.

I give up lookin' for signs, and I start taking in my surroundings. Honestly, it's more likely I'll see or hear the dog. It's real quiet out here. The only sounds are the crunch of sticks under our boots, and the occasional caw of a crow.

A half hour or so in, the snow starts fallin'. Big, wet flakes. Weatherman's calling for three to six inches, and my gut says it'll be closer to three. Good news. About a year ago, Mona bought herself a little tin can. It's a piece of crap. No ground clearance. No weight to it. And she rides her tires bald.

Once, I had to slash her front right tire—I smashed a bottle in the road so she'd think she ran over glass—to get her to go buy a new one before she ended up hydroplaning and killin' herself.

My gut aches like it always does when I think about Mona. She's soft. Soft-hearted. Getting a little soft around the middle these days, too, but it looks good on her.

She looks out for other people, but she don't take care of herself. At least that's what it seems like from a distance.

She hasn't spoken to me since she said, "Get out." Four years ago now. A few days after that night, she sent me an email about how it hurt too bad to look at me, my stuff's on the porch, and she'd find herself an apartment and clear out.

I told her stay in the house, we're underwater on the mortgage, selling don't make sense.

The part about the mortgage was a lie. We had plenty of equity in the house, but Mona didn't do the bills. She didn't know.

She cuts me a check for six hundred bucks each month. She writes *rent* in the memo line. It's the only contact she'll have with me. She still don't know that the mortgage is nearly two thousand. I deposit the check straight into a savings account.

She'd probably be pissed if she knew. She's real self-sufficient. She was a CNA when we were together, but she went to night school on the nursing home's dime, and now she's an LPN. The wife of an old buddy from Smoke and Steel works with Mona, and I hear about her through the grapevine.

Suddenly, Heavy stops in his tracks and raises his fist. He gestures due north with two fingers. It takes a minute, but I make out the movement in the underbrush that caught his eye. Damn, if his phone ain't still in his hand.

We hold our breaths and stalk closer. There's a rustling of leaves, and then a gray streak skitters off.

"Squirrel." I exhale.

"Squirrel," Heavy agrees. "How long we been out here?"

"Hour or so."

He sighs. "I should get back. Work's stacking up."

I don't know how he does it. The man owns none of his own time. "Go on. I'm gonna keep lookin'."

He nods, but he hangs with me for a spell in a small clearing, our necks craned up. Tall pines sway above us, the snow catching on the needles. It's like the sky's a snow globe, fat flakes falling down but not reaching where we stand.

"I could live out here," he says. "'The heavens declare the glory of God; the skies proclaim the work of his hands.'"

"Amen." Our brothers think it's a quirk that Heavy has, quoting the Good Book. His faith is as large as the man, though. You watch what he does, you'll see it. *He is truly his brother's keeper and the finder of lost children.*

After Mona cut me loose, I went on a six-month bender.

Drink, drugs, women. I was blacking out. I had to delete Mona's number from my phone so I didn't call her up, say something to hurt her worse. Then one day, Heavy finds me passed out in clubhouse yard after a party. He offers me a job. Says quit the firehouse and patch in to Steel Bones. He saved my life that day. I got sober, and I haven't had a woman or a toke since.

"I'd build a cabin up there." Heavy tilts his head toward the low mountains in the far distance. "You ever think about walking away from it all?"

I shake my head. "Nope. What I want ain't out there."

He slides me a knowing look. "You know, a man makes a mistake, he shouldn't have to pay for it all the days of his life."

"Yeah. All the same, I'll wait on Mona."

Pity fills his eyes. "It's been years, my friend."

I shrug. "I ain't got nothin' else goin' on. I'll wait."

He strokes his bushy-ass beard. "I guess I don't get it."

So, I put it in terms he can understand. "You know that Bobber you and Charge rehabbed when you was kids?"

He grins. "Of course."

"It's a rusted piece of shit. You ever gonna junk it?"

His grin widens. "Nope. It's gonna take up space in the garage, and you assholes are gonna bitch about it forever."

"Yup." My point's made.

Heavy rubs his hands and blows on them. He ain't wearin' gloves, and the temperatures gone down a good ten degrees. "Did you just compare to your ex to a 'rusted piece of shit?'"

"She ain't here. I stand by it."

He chuckles, dips his chin, and heads back for the club-house. We've managed to get a good distance from civilization. When the sound of his boots fade, the silence swells until there's almost a weight to it.

Mona would like it out here. She ain't exactly outdoorsy —I never could get her to go camping—but if there's a public restroom nearby, she loves bein' outside. I took her to Lake Patonquin and hiking along the Luckahannock many times.

I rub my chest. I miss her. Every day, but especially times like this when there's something pretty to see. Mona's got a round face, plain brown hair. She doesn't like her nose, thinks it's too pointy. She doesn't like her eyebrows, either. Or her chin for some reason. Her mother did a number on her, convincing her that she ain't much to look at.

She's gorgeous, though. Her body's smokin' hot. And when she sees something pretty, and she smiles? Her whole damn face lights up. Everybody around can't help but smile, too. Most beautiful thing I ever saw.

It took me no time at all to ruin that smile, to make it so I never get to see it shinin' at me again.

One night. One hour. Not even. More like twenty minutes, truth be told.

You ever watch a kid spend forever stacking blocks, and then he knocks it over? That look on his face 'cause he can't quite believe you can ruin something with such a small fraction of the effort it took to build it?

I think about that a lot. How little intent and forethought it takes to destroy things.

But honestly? The sad truth is Mona's smiles were few and far between long before the night I fucked everything up. The losses broke her before I did.

We started trying for a baby as soon as I landed the job with the Shady Gap Fire Department. I'm one of five—big, happy Catholic family—and Mona's an only child. A lonely one, the way she tells it. We wanted a full house.

I got her pregnant the first month of trying. We called the little guy Peanut. And we lost him—or her—at ten weeks.

We tried again. Bam. Pregnant. We lost Jellybean at eight weeks. I said we should take a break. Give her body a rest. But before we made any concrete decision, she was expecting again. And third time's a charm, right?

We cleared the twelve-week mark. Mona's smile started peeking out again here and there. We started calling the baby Lemon after the size chart at the obstetrician, found out she was a girl at the ultrasound. We lost her right after, over Labor Day weekend. Almost eighteen weeks.

Mona broke. She'd been bouncing back, and then one day, she just stayed down. And for the life of me, I couldn't figure out how to get her back up again.

Then, I did what I did. I wasn't the kid who knocked the blocks over. I was the kid who crushed the block under his boot.

It ain't an easy thing to live with. Knowing that about yourself. That you done that to a person. The woman you loved. That you could then sink even lower.

I sniff and take a gander around. It's growing late, and even with the snow's reflection, it's getting hard to see through the undergrowth. Maybe it's time to call it a day.

I turn and begin the trek back home. Soon enough, the sun sets, the snow eases off, and a full moon hangs low and bright.

I'm almost back to the clubhouse when my phone rings. I fish it from my bib pocket.

"Yeah?"

Heavy's voice booms into the silent night. "Check your

messages. I just forwarded you a picture of the dog from Deb."

I check it out, and I can't stop the snort of laughter. "Holy shit. Is that a coyote?"

"Yup."

"We was lookin' to rescue a coyote?"

"Seems like it."

I enlarge the picture. "That don't look nothin' like a German Shepherd."

"If you squint, kind of tilt your head..." Heavy's crackin' up.

"All right, brother. I'll be back in thirty."

"We'll leave the light on."

It's so bright, with the moon on the snow, I make it back in good time. I grab Shirlene's chair and dump the baggie of dry food I brought next to the dumpster. No sense in it goin' to waste. If the coyote runs from people, he likely ain't rabid.

I take Shirlene's chair to the garage, spray a little Rust-Oleum on it. Then I head down to the basement gym to lift. It's leg day.

I'll probably do five miles or so on the treadmill after. If I'm not dead tired, it's hard to fall asleep when I hit the sheets.

Mona ain't there anymore.

The bed's too cold.

## 3

### MONA

In retrospect, I probably should have waited until later to pay Miss Janice's grandson a visit. It's ten o'clock in the morning, but clearly, he's not the rise-and-shine type.

There's no longer a ceramic frog or a flowerbed in the front lawn. There are green shards and cigarette butts in a mud puddle with bent, plastic edging. Of course, no one has shoveled the walk, so I pick my way carefully. It's really slippery in places.

There's a car in the drive, and someone shuffling around inside, but no one's answered the door. I heard the doorbell ring, and the Venetian blinds fluttered. That was about three minutes ago. I knocked, too, to be sure. Very friendly.

The blinds part again. I wave. Yup, I'm still here. Freezing my butt off.

"Janice sent me." I aim to sound confident, casual. "She needs something."

More shuffling.

Okay. Maybe the grandson has houseguests. "Is Tommy home?"

I'm sure this isn't going to end with me getting the ring, but the kid can at least tell me "no" to my face. Little rat. Miss Janice would have a conniption if she saw the empty beer bottles lined up on the porch railing.

I knock again. Less friendly. "I just need to talk to you about Janice Merrill!"

The door flies open, and I barely catch myself in time before I tumble inside. Good thing, too. Tommy Merrill is a skinny kid, and I've never been intimidated by him before, but he looks downright sinister when no one else is around.

He's emaciated, probably due to the drugs, and he has gauges in his ears and baggy jeans hanging below his dingy boxers. He's scratching his bare chest with dirt-crusted fingernails.

"What the fuck you want, lady?"

Welp, there goes my good attitude. I grit my teeth and force a smile. "I'm Mona Wall, a friend of your grandmother. She sent me here to get her engagement ring."

"Get the fuck outta here. You ain't stealin' from me with no bullshit story."

"You can call Shady Acres and speak to your grandmother. She asked me to get the ring since you forgot it the last time you came to visit." I feel stupid, like a prissy schoolmarm.

"The fuck you say." He sniffs, and his gaze darts over my shoulder to the street. Checking to see if I brought anyone with me. I didn't.

And Five Constantine Court is at the end of the road. Last night's snow brought the temperature down, and there's no one outside.

He shuffles forward, crowding me. I step back, and somehow, I end up pressed against the porch railing.

He slowly licks his lips. "You want Mee Maw's ring? What's it worth to you?"

His breath reeks of tortilla chips and nicotine.

"I'm not paying you for the ring. It belongs to your grandmother. It means a lot to her. If you don't have it anymore, just say so."

"Oh, I got the ring. It's upstairs. How 'bout you come in? I'll show it to you?" He's leering, and he takes another step closer until we're almost chest to chest.

"Please back up." I say it firmly, so I don't know why the words come out of my mouth all squeaky and weak.

"I tell you what, Mama. Come on upstairs, and I'll let you work for it. I don't usually go for fatties with that desperate stink, but, hey, since you deliver...I'll throw you a pity fuck."

Then he smirks, his stained, yellow teeth inches from my mouth, and I shove him, smack in the middle of his skinny chest, and I run for my car.

Of course, instead of heading through the fresh snow in the front yard, I instinctively take the walk, which has melted and refrozen, so I'm slipping and sliding, and he's laughing. Another man joins him on the porch, a bigger, rougher-looking guy, and there's a woman, too. They're all laughing.

And then I hit a slick patch, and my feet sail out from under me. Thud. I land flat on my tailbone, and I bite my tongue, drawing blood. My eyes burn, and then of course, I burst out in hot tears.

"Look at that dumb bitch. Awww, she fell." The woman cackles.

"Hey, don't leave. We was just starting to have some fun," Tommy calls. "Is it 'cause I called you fat? I take it back. You ain't fat, you jiggly."

My face is hot and wet, and my lungs burn from sprinting in the cold. I slam my car door, and I fumble at the seat belt. I can't see through the tears. I can hear their muffled laughter, and then a snowball hits my passenger-side window.

My hands are shaking so badly that I can't get the key in the ignition. Tommy and the other man lope across the front lawn—oh shit, oh shit—and then one of them kicks the side of my car. There's gonna be a dent.

I scramble for the locks, but they engaged automatically. I almost accidentally *unlock* the doors. There's so much shouting, and my pounding blood is deafening in my ears.

"That's right! Get gone! And remember I know where you work! Maybe I'll pay *you* a visit! Dumb bitch!"

Finally, the key slides home, and I peel off, fishtailing in the ice as I burst into full-blown hysterics.

That little *asshole.*

I should turn around and run his scrawny ass over with my car.

Or should I call the cops? I don't want to call the cops. How would that conversation go?

*Yes, officer, I was just chased off someone's property by a kid who called me a fatty, threw snowballs, and kicked my car. What was I doing there? Trying to get a diamond ring from a druggie.*

I check the rearview mirror. My face is bright, mottled red, and I'm not sure what's winning: the terror, the humiliation, or the fury.

If I were a big man, that *never* would have happened.

I'm flying down route 29, pounding on the steering wheel, head throbbing with swelling fury and the aftermath of fear, and I realize two things. I need to slow down. I'm going eighty and black ice is a definite possibility. And I'm heading toward Petty's Mill.

John lives in Petty's Mill. That's where I send my rent checks. To the Steel Bones Clubhouse. I have a vague memory of where it is. I'm probably fifteen minutes away.

I haven't seen or spoken to John in four years.

I hate him. He's the boogeyman of my life. I put him—all of that—behind me. He cheated on me at the lowest point in my life, and then he swanned away.

But he's a big man. *Really* big.

And Steel Bones isn't a leisure club like Smoke and Steel. They're the real deal. Not quite one percenters, but no one in this county messes with them.

The grip of my hysterics begins to ease, the tears ebb, and I suck down a deep breath. The meaty part of my palm is sore from beating on the car.

Am I really going to go crying to John Wall?

If I showed him the dent in my car door, I bet he'd help me. He hates it when people destroy public property, litter, stuff like that. He was raised really strict. And if I told him what Tommy said...he'd handle it. The Walls are old-fashioned. None of them would ever stand for a man threatening a woman.

But can I stand owing John Wall anything?

This is a bad idea.

But I'm already pulling into the parking lot in front of the Steel Bones clubhouse and parking in an empty spot. I run my fingers through my hair, but with the static, it's hopeless. I tug on a gray knit hat that Miss Janice made me. It doesn't help that I look like a depressed Hershey's Kiss, my face is splotchy, and what am I wearing? A red parka, mom jeans, and rubber boots.

Oh, this is a terrible idea. He's going to take one look at me and think I've lost my mind. I've got so much adrenaline still racing through my veins, I don't feel quite right. I should maybe push pause, take a few deep breaths.

*Fatty. Desperate stink. Pity fuck.*

I should go get the rifle John insisted on leaving in the house and shoot all those beer cans off that...that...*asshole's* porch railing. And if he comes outside, I should shoot straight through those stupid holes in his earlobes.

Nope. No. This is a better idea than that.

I summon all my courage—which is ninety-nine percent humiliated indignation—and I traipse across the asphalt past every make and model of big truck you can imagine. Guess the MC's bikes are in the garage for winter.

Even though it's hardly eleven in the morning, there's hard rock spilling from the front doors. I'm not sure how this works—if this clubhouse is more like a bar or a private club or a business—but there's no way anyone would hear me knock.

I throw my shoulder into sliding open the massive, wooden doors enough to slip through. The clubhouse is an old garage with a vaulted roof and a modern glass-and-steel annex attached in the back. The doors are in the original part, probably from the 1930s or 1940s, well-oiled, but *heavy*.

Whoa.

The instant I step into the common room, I feel...obvious.

Three grizzled men swivel in their bar stools to gawk at me. One is at least four hundred pounds. Another is missing both of his legs. And the third guy kind of looks like a graying Superman who's tanned himself with cigarette smoke.

There's a woman on a leather couch, passed out on her stomach with a hot pink spandex dress bunched around her waist. She's wearing a black thong. No one seems to be paying any attention to her.

Two shirtless men are playing pool while a shirtless woman watches, sitting cross-legged on top of a table, swigging liquor from the bottle. She has really firm boobs.

The woman in the thong has a really firm butt.

What am I doing here?

"Hey, lady. You lost?" A younger man in a black vest that reads "Prospect" calls out from where he's picking up empties and dumping them in an overstuffed trash bag.

I straighten my spine. "I need to see John Wall."

"Who?" the young guy asks. "Ain't no John here."

One of the men playing pool, a guy with a shaved head and tattoos covering every inch of visible skin, strides over, cue still in his hand.

"She wants Wall." He jerks his chin at the prospect, and he takes off, presumably to find my ex.

"You're Mona, right?"

He knows my name? Maybe from the return address on the rent checks.

"Yeah. Sorry to, uh, interrupt."

"No problem, babe. I'm Creech." He offers me a hand. I squeeze it quickly. He grins, flashing a gold tooth next to a missing incisor. "You want a drink?"

"Oh. No. It's, um, too early." I blush when I see he's pulled a flask from his pocket. "Oh, but you, uh, feel free. Don't mind me."

"I always feel free, babe. You sure? Looks like you could use it." He raises the flask and winks.

You know what? I hold out my hand. He chuckles and passes me the flask.

I take a sip, and my nose tickles.

"Oh, cinnamon schnapps!" I haven't had this since I was in high school.

"Tastes like hard candies, don't it?"

I'm about to agree, but a door at the far end of the cavernous hall bangs open, and a gargantuan man storms through.

It's John.

And John is *huge*.

He was always a big guy, tall and stocky with a beer belly, but now? He's the Hulk. Hercules. Conan the Barbarian. He must be some kind of bodybuilder.

Under my bulky winter coat, I suck in my gut.

He strides over, and the floor doesn't shake, but it's easy to imagine it does.

His neck has muscles. His biceps are so pronounced, his arms don't touch his sides.

He's wearing a plain black T-shirt, and I don't think it's cut tight, I think he's that swole. He's sweaty, and he's wearing white athletic shorts—which are designed baggy but cling to his massive thighs—so maybe I interrupted him working out.

Hah. *Of course*, he was working out. I've spent the last four years losing a battle to the same thirty pounds, and he turned himself into a comic book hero.

I hate this man. I *hate* him.

"Mona? What's wrong?"

Then he's looming above me, solid as, well, a wall, and he smells like clean sweat and pine trees, for some reason. Not like disinfectant, but like the outdoors. He *smells* good. Butterflies flap in my stomach, a whole herd of them.

My gaze flies around the room. The woman in the thong has roused, and she's watching us as she lights a cigarette. The woman with her boobs out is shooting me an ugly look.

I still have the tattooed man's flask in my hand.

This was a terrible idea.

"I should—" I look around wildly until I find the tattooed man leaning on a nearby high table. I skirt around John and hand the man his flask. "I should go."

But somehow, I've ventured further into the clubhouse, and now John is between me and the exit.

"Mona, what happened?"

His voice is just like I remember. Just like on the voicemails from when we were happy that I've never gotten the courage to delete. Gruff. Deep. Calm.

I don't feel calm at all. This coat is hot, sweat's trickling down my back, and my forehead's itching under this knit cap.

Everyone's gawking. The men at the bar. The women. Did John sleep with either of them? Is the one who's giving me the evil eye his girlfriend? The butterflies turn to nausea.

"Go get her a bottle of water," John barks at the prospect. "Mona, can I take your coat?"

My eyes fly to his. They're a warm brown. Nice. Concerned. I take a steadying breath.

Who cares if he's slept with these women? We're not together anymore. I came for a reason. I'm here now. I can do this.

"Can we, um, go somewhere and talk? With, uh, less people?"

"Of course, b—" He was going to call me *baby*. That's what he called me. And I called him *hon*. "Yeah. How about my room?"

Oh, crap. I wasn't suggesting that. I don't want to see his bed. Where he sleeps with other women. Like the one sitting on top of the table, swinging her legs—tanned golden brown in the middle of winter—and glaring at me with her boobs out.

I guess he reads my face. "Or we could go outside. There's a fire pit. It's not that cold." The prospect bounds over with a bottled water. John takes it and presses it in my hand. "Come on. It's this way."

He leads me across the common room. The view of his back is almost as impressive as his front. It's like following a bear. With really tight buns. He still has that bubble butt.

John takes me down a hall, and at an open door, he says, "Wait here."

He pauses like he's making sure I stay put. Sheesh. I'm not going to spy on his secret biker club. I roll my eyes. His brow furrows, but then he nods and ducks into a room, emerging with a bright orange jacket. I don't think it's his. The arms are tight, and he can't zip it.

"Here we are." He ushers me through a back door into a snow-covered yard. It's huge. There's a picnic pavilion, a small covered stage, and what looks like a jungle gym for kids made of tractor tires. My heart twinges. I shove the ache down, lock it away.

John leads me over to a fire pit surrounded by logs. He brushes off the snow. "You cold? I can make a fire."

This is so surreal.

"No. It's fine."

I take the seat he offers. I'm actually hot. All my feelings have gotten trapped in my polyester coat, and I'm sweating my butt off.

"Shit. You need a glass for your water?" He rises, but I shake my head.

"No. It's fine. I shouldn't have come here. I'm sorry."

He frowns. "No, you come here whenever you want. What's wrong, Mona?"

I don't know how to react to the first statement, so I answer the question.

"It's...stupid. I still work at Shady Acres, you know?" I pause. He's listening. This doesn't seem like news to him.

"There's a woman there named Miss Janice. She's real sweet, and she's helped me out in the past. Anyway, her grandson won't bring her engagement ring. He probably hocked it. He's an *asshole*."

John will know what I mean. I rarely cuss. He nods somberly. He gets it.

"I went to get the ring this morning, and he—"

For the first time, it occurs to me that I might want to tread carefully. Before John decided he was done with me and had sex with a firefighter groupie, he was always very protective. If Tommy Merrill tried that when we were together? John would kill him. No doubt in my mind.

"What did he do?" John's tone is a full octave deeper. Growlier.

"He wouldn't give me the ring."

John stares at me, his head cocked slightly to the side. He doesn't believe that's the whole truth. I press my lips together.

"That why you've been crying? 'Cause he wouldn't give you the ring?"

My fingers fly to my face. My eyes are puffy and tender. "I got very frustrated."

"So frustrated that you come talk to me for the first time in four years?"

There's bitterness in his voice. My jaw tightens. He doesn't have the right to be bitter.

If he wanted to talk to me, he's had plenty of time. The phone works two ways. I clamber to my feet. The snow's turned to slush out here, and I slip a little.

John stands, steadying me with a firm grip on my elbow. "I'm sorry. I didn't mean it to sound that way. I'm glad you came."

He is?

"Come on. Sit back down. Tell me about this punk."

He kind of guides me back down, but this time, he sits me right next to him, no space between us on the log. I wish I could suck in my thighs. Mine splay, pressing against his. His are rock hard.

I scooch away. He widens his stance until we're touching again.

He always did take up as much room as he wanted. On the couch, he had two cushions. I had one. He commandeered three quarters of our bed.

My breath catches. I don't need to be thinking about our bed. What was the question?

"Tommy Merrill? He's in his early twenties. A real jerk. He's completely trashed his grandmother's house. I'm sure he's pawned the ring, or traded it for drugs. And she's the best. She's been kind to me."

John pins me with a stare. I can't quite read it, but it's not unfriendly. Maybe he'd do this favor for me. I'm here. No harm in asking.

"I guess I was thinking...maybe we could go back together and ask for the ring. You could kind of hang back. Just seeing you, I think, he'd take me more seriously. I could, um...pay you or something."

"Pay me?" His voice is clipped.

"Yeah. For your time."

He tilts his head back and stares up at the gray sky, his huge hands resting motionless on his massive knees. He's thinking of a polite way to say get lost. I'm sure of it. This was a mistake.

I should've at least had a plan. I can't actually afford to pay him. At least, not much.

A goose honks way overhead. Poor fellow's lost. He should be down south by now. I know how he must feel. I'm totally out of my element here.

"Okay," John finally says.

"Okay?"

"Yeah. But I don't want your money." He lowers his eyes to mine. "I want something else."

The butterflies go nuts again. Is he going to ask for sex? Of course not. That only happens in romance novels. To women who aren't wearing handmade, crocheted hats and muck boots.

And I wouldn't have sex with him anyway. He cheated on me. He didn't even try to hide it. And I'm still not sure if that makes him a bigger jerk or not.

My face is burning; I'm gnawing at my lower lip. John waits, cool, calm, and collected.

"What do you want?" I finally sputter.

"Dinner."

I blink.

"Home-cooked dinner. Meatloaf. Mashed potatoes, not from the box. Green beans. Dessert."

He wants me to cook dinner? He always did like my meatloaf, but it's nothing special. I got the recipe from the back of a soup can. I'm not sure what to say.

"Green beans are out of season. The ones in the store are all spindly."

"Green beans from a can are fine."

Seriously? He's feeding *that body* canned vegetables? "You'll go with me to get the ring if I make you dinner?"

"No."

My insides drop.

"You're not going anywhere near this guy again. I'll go get the ring. You make dinner. Get those brown-and-serve rolls, too."

"That's a lot of carbs."

"I can handle the carbs." His lips twitch. Then he reaches out and flicks the pom-pom on top of my knit cap. "I like your hat."

My face burns. Jerk. I know it's a stupid-looking hat. It has a tassel, for goodness' sake. Does he think he looks all that in bright orange? Shit. He does look amazing.

I stare at my hands in my lap. John nudges me with his thigh. It's quiet except for the muffled music coming from the clubhouse.

I breathe out, close my eyes for a second, collect myself. John's never been cruel on purpose. If you don't count that last night when he came home late. He's teasing me. I'm just not used to it anymore.

"Thanks. I like your coat."

"This old thing." He grins, and tries to tug it closed, but there's a good inch-wide gap. "I do get a lot of attention in it."

"Helps when you land the airplanes, eh?"

"Or when you need an emergency cone, yeah. Comes in handy."

I can't help but smile, but the good feeling fades quickly. We're left sitting next to each other on a log in the bitter cold, awkward and lost for words.

"What if I said forget about it?" I keep my eyes glued on an outbuilding. A bird has left tracks winding all over the snow on its roof.

"I'd still get you that ring. Then you'd feel guilty and make me dinner anyway."

"Inevitable, is it?"

"Yup."

Even though I'm sitting firmly on my butt, I feel unsteady. How did I get here? The drive's a blur. I don't think I've ever been that out-of-my-mind in my life. I was driving on instinct, and I came here. Such a huge decision, and I didn't think about it for even a second.

I've done a good job of getting over John Wall. There were days early on when I couldn't breathe. I remember collapsing on the floor in the bedroom and *bawling*, hating myself 'cause I couldn't pull myself together.

That was a long time ago now.

Why would I let him back in? Even for a dinner? I don't need to make peace with him. I've been managing fine alone. Doing good, actually. Making something of myself.

He's absolutely quiet and still while my brain whirrs. I open the water and take a sip so it's not so weird, sitting here in silence.

He's not asking for sex. Or a second chance. He wants dinner.

Maybe he wants to bury the hatchet, come to a place where we're not friends, but we're friendly. That would make the whole "landlord" situation easier. I've had to scrounge money when the toilet clogs or a shingle gets blown off the roof. If we were on speaking terms, I could let him know, deduct the cost of repairs out of the rent. That would be a great help.

Maybe I'm making excuses.

Heck, it's just dinner. I was going to make something anyway. Might as well make meatloaf. I don't need to go to the store. I have all the ingredients at home. I'd only have to defrost the ground beef.

He's doing me a favor. I can do one for him. It doesn't have to be more than that.

An ugly voice inside me snarls, "Why would you do *that man* any favors?" My bitter side. She had a lot to say when John and I first split.

I sigh. I don't like my bitter side. She makes me feel worse. Like I'm a sucker and a loser, *and* I'm spiteful besides.

Hell. It's only meatloaf. "All right. When?"

He answers instantly. "Tonight."

"Okay."

"Okay?"

"Yeah." I remember the other man, the scarier one. "Be careful when you go. Tommy had another man with him. There was a girl, too. The other guy was a real shady character."

"Might could take me, could he?"

I slide John a glance. His lip is kicked up at the corner. He knows he's as big as a linebacker.

"Take someone with you anyway. I think he's just a punk kid, but if he's high..." Crap. What if he has a gun? What if there are more guys at his house now? Maybe this isn't a good idea.

John lays a heavy hand on my knee. "I'll be careful. I'll take a few brothers. Ask around beforehand. I'm sure we know his crew somehow. It's a small town. No worries." He squeezes, and then he takes his hand away.

My knee is warm, warmer than it should be from such a brief touch. I stare for a few seconds at the muddy slush around the snow-dusted fire pit.

"Thank you, John."

An errant gust of wind stirs up the snow, flinging crystals to tickle my nose. Closer to the clubhouse a door slams, and a woman shrieks with laughter.

After a long moment, John says, "Your chocolate cake would be nice for dessert."

Then he stands, walks me to the parking lot the long way, around the building instead of through, and opens the door of my car. He can barely wedge his bulk in between my little economy-sized vehicle and the truck next to it.

"What's this?" He's noticed the dent Tommy Merrill left in the side. There's suspicion in his voice.

"Bird." It's the first thing I can think of. He seems serious enough about dealing with Tommy. I don't want him to go in with guns blazing.

"Bird?"

"Yup. A bird flew into my car." I'm a terrible liar.

"Like the Road Runner?" Of course, John doesn't believe me. His mouth is turned down, but his eyes are twinkling. My traitorous belly flips.

"Meep, meep." I click my seat belt and ease into reverse. "What time tonight?"

"Eight."

"Okay."

He gently shuts the door and steps back. In my rearview, I see him watch me until I pull out onto the highway, a giant in clingy white shorts and a neon-orange puffy jacket, towering in a parking lot full of oversized trucks.

He looks amazing.

Larger than life.

I'm in so much trouble.

# 4

## WALL

"They chased her to her car." Forty squats, eyeing the tracks in the snow.

I figured that out already. This fucker's gonna die. Snowplow hasn't come through, yet, so you can see the tire marks where Mona fishtailed as she bolted.

This fucker's gonna die slow.

I tighten my grip on the pipe wrench. I've got my piece in a side holster, but for close quarters, I prefer hand tools.

Grinder's got himself a tire iron. I don't think it's a matter of preference for him so much as what was in the back of his truck. We're lucky he didn't roll up with an empty whiskey bottle.

Forty's probably packing a semi-automatic with a scope and a bowie knife in his boot. You can't take the Rangers out of the man. He's obsessed with his gear.

"What's the plan?" Grinder hocks and spits.

"Mikey's out back. Grinder, you and Forty bust down the side door. I go in the front. We flush whoever's in there out the back. Forty clears upstairs."

Grinder knits his thick, gray brows. "I know I ain't as fit

as I once was, but ain't Mikey about a hundred twenty pounds soakin' wet?"

"We gave him the RPG."

Grinder busts out in a guffaw. "You didn't give that boy actual grenades, did you?"

"How's the boy gonna become a man if we coddle him?" Forty stands, brushing snow off his perfectly pressed cargo pants.

"On three?" I don't want to stand here gabbing any longer. Every second this takes is a second away from Mona. She came to me. She *finally* came to me.

The hardest thing I ever did was stand in the parking lot and let her drive away. I need to get this ring, put this little asshole on ice until I have time to deal with him, and then go to my woman.

God, why couldn't it have been this simple this whole time? Find the ring, kill the asshole, get the girl. It's like a video game.

My brain knows it's nowhere near a done deal, but my body is beyond ready. I've been sporting a semi for hours, and my adrenaline's surging. I'm bouncing on my toes. In a few hours, I'm gonna be alone with Mona. *Finally*.

Grinder's lookin' at me funny. "All right, son. You call it."

"One. Two. Three!" We break.

Forty sprints around the house, Grinder lagging several feet behind. He's almost sixty, and his workouts consist of drinking beers while he spots me as I lift. He wanted to come, though. Change of scenery.

When I calculate that Forty must be close to his mark, I charge the front door. The original plan was to knock, but when I saw the tracks in the snow, plans changed.

I kick down the door and rush in, shouting, "Tommy Merrill! You are dead, motherfucker!"

Three young dudes blink at me from a sofa. Two have videogame controllers in their hands. The third has a bong.

Forty sails past me up the stairs. Grinder blocks the exit to the kitchen, huffing and puffing.

"Which one of you is Tommy Merrill?"

The two playing video games look at the third, a scrawny guy with gauges. There's a brief pause, then he gently sets down his bong, pitches the remote control at me full force— missing by several feet—and scrambles over the back of the sofa.

He dashes for Grinder. I guess he don't see the tire iron.

There's a thwack, a crack, and then Tommy Merrill is writhing on the filthy carpet, clutching his stomach, moaning.

Grinder twirls his weapon. "Steee-rike!"

Forty clumps down the stairs. "Second level is all clear."

The prospect races in, launcher over his shoulder, warhead in his hand. "What's goin' on? No one came out."

"Well, that's anticlimactic," Forty says.

"Holy shit. Is that an RPG?" a guy from the sofa asks. A damp spot spreads in the crotch of his friend's shorts, and the smell of piss fills the room.

I head for our boy Tommy, and Forty takes my place in the gaping hole where the front door used to be. I'll have to fix that later, just in case the old lady still owns the house.

Tommy's a skinny guy, but he's got some height on him and the stringy muscles of an addict who spends a lot of time hustling. He's more than big enough to intimidate a woman like Mona. Mona ain't never hurt a fly.

I drive my boot into his ribs, and he screams.

Mona shouldn't have come within twenty yards of a piece of trash like this, and she rolled up here knockin' on his door? My heart's stuck in my throat, and I can't swallow it back down.

"Where's your granny's ring, dumbass?"

"I don't know what you're talkin' about, man!"

Guess Tommy's a "hard way" kind of guy. I drag him up and prop him on his feet. Then, I release my hands. He gives almost immediately and crashes to the floor. For good measure, I nudge his side with my toe, and he sobs.

"Stop, man, stop!"

"Where's the ring?"

"I don't have it no more! I sold it!"

Figures. "Who'd you sell it to?"

"I don't know!"

This guy. I groan. "Can I borrow that?" I nod at Grinder's tire iron. It's got a little more heft than my wrench. He shrugs and hands it over. I stomp over to Tommy's media center.

He's got a sweet setup. Sound bar and a subwoofer. The latest consoles. Eighty-six-inch TV.

I start with the speakers. Whack. Whack. They go crashing into the wall.

"Strike two!" Grinder hoots.

"Man, no!" Tommy's dragged himself to his feet again in a desperate bid to save his shit. He lurches forward just as I drive the tire iron into a console. I wail on it until it's nothing but parts and twisted plastic.

Grinder grabs Tommy in a bear hug to hold him back. I raise the iron, line it up with the television.

"Who'd you sell that ring to, Tommy?"

"Oh, man. Oh, man." He's pasty white and sweating like a pig.

I give him a second to make a decision. On the one hand, I know how unnatural it feels for a guy like Tommy to tell the truth. On the other hand, the TV *is* a Samsung. This has gotta be a tough one for him.

"All right, then." I draw back, elbow up.

"Ethan Eckels!" Tommy moans, as if he can't believe he's giving up the name. "He ain't gonna have it no more. It was a trade. Weeks ago. That thing's long gone, man. I'll pay you for it. I just need a few days. Don't touch the TV, man."

I catch Forty's eye. We know the name Ethan Eckels.

Matter of fact, we ran that pissant dealer out of Petty's Mill a few months back. He deals in meth, fentanyl, nasty shit. As a rule, Steel Bones don't concern itself with what any grown man chooses to put in his own body, but our business demands discretion. We don't need Feds in town or the local mothers up in arms.

I guess Ethan Eckels didn't stay gone. Heavy'll be interested to hear this, but Forty's gonna have to tell him. I'm due home for dinner.

The thought warms my chest. I almost don't send the tire iron into the television.

"Where's Ethan Eckels?" I ask.

There's snot running down Tommy's face. "I don't know, man. I don't know!"

Oh, well. I tee up and let 'er fly. Nail the screen right in the center. Sparks fly.

"Asshole!" Tommy screams, straining against Grinder's grip.

"Guess we're gonna have to break his kneecaps." Grinder throws Tommy into his friends on the sofa like the world's wobbliest bowling ball.

"I don't know." I pick up that pretty glass water pipe. Excellent workmanship. A one-of-a-kind piece.

What kind of person can't be bothered to vacuum the carpet and spends hundreds of bucks on a bong? A connoisseur, I'd say. I dangle the pipe over the coffee table and cock my head.

"He's crashing here. In Shady Gap. At his woman's place on Main Street." Tommy wheezes and whimpers through his confession as he holds up his hands. "I can show you where. Put it down, man."

I let it fall. Glass shatters. He cries out. First time he's sounded human.

"Take him to the cabin," I tell Grinder. "But drive him down Main Street first. Have him point out the girlfriend's place. He gives you any trouble, let the prospect use him for target practice."

"Oh, gee, boss, seriously?" Mikey's stroking the launcher. It's gonna be hard to pry that out of his hands.

"We'll see." Forty slaps him on the back. "What should we do with the witnesses?"

The two friends are huddled on the sofa, makin' themselves as small as possible. We got a procedure for bystanders and eyewitnesses that along with our reputation, has served us well.

"Do you know who we are?" I ask the guy who pissed himself.

"Yeah. Yes. Your S—"

I hold up my palm. "Uh, uh, uh. No names. Did you see anything?"

"No. No, sir."

"What about you?" I ask the one that's turning an alarming shade of green. Back in my firefighting days, I would have been calling for a barf bag.

"Nothing. Sir."

I hold my hand out. "Wallets, please."

They don't move immediately, so Grinder hoists his tire

iron. There are two wallets on the coffee table a split-second later.

I dig out the licenses and snap a pic of their home addresses. Both are local boys. One's a cousin to Creech, I believe.

"Okay, we're gonna leave now. You two are gonna stay here until this house is clean. *Pristine.* Hang that door back up. And for chrissake, pick up every single beer can from that front porch. Capisce?"

The guys nod enthusiastically.

"Mikey, why don't you and the RPG stay to supervise. Think you can handle that?"

"Absolutely." Mikey flops down on an easy chair and props the weapon on his shoulder, using the back of the chair as a brace.

"Ain't that a picture," Grinder says.

"Our boy." I slap Grinder's back as Forty and I stroll out the hole where the front door used to be.

Forty heads for his Jeep so we can move it into the garage and load Tommy up unseen. It's almost six o'clock. I need to shower and shave before I head over to Shady Gap. My stomach rumbles, and my cock aches. This was fun, but my heart ain't in it anymore.

"Can you take care of this from here?" I ask.

Forty nods. "I'll talk to Heavy. He'll want to move on Eckels. Dude seems to have a thick head. Might need to be cracked open."

"It can wait until tomorrow, yeah?"

Forty's our VP, so if he decides this needs handling right now, that's gonna leave me in an uncomfortable position. As it is, my jeans have been chafing my stiff dick all damn day.

"Yeah. It can wait. You headed over to Mona's?"

"After I clean up."

Forty flashes me a half-smile. "Good luck, brother."

"I need it."

Mona's got no reason to forgive me. It's been four years, but the basic facts of the matter haven't changed. She was hurting, and in a moment of weakness, I slept with another woman. She kicked me out, and instead of fighting for her, I lost my damn mind.

Some women forgive a man a dozen times for doing what I did. They'll ignore it for years. Lord knows Ernestine's been putting up with Grinder's shit since the eighties.

Mona's not like that. But she's got a warm, loving heart.

Maybe she would give a man a chance. If he really changed. If he showed her that's he's all in.

That's all I need. One chance.

That's what my whole heart is ridin' on.

## 5

## MONA

I t would've been really desperate to get my hair cut this afternoon. Earlier today, John couldn't see my hair under that dumb hat, so he wouldn't know that I went to the salon and got a trim—maybe just a blowout—but *I'd* know.

I glare at the mirror.

Well, I have my pride, and I also have split ends. I'm going to have to live with it. As it is, I spent the afternoon on the treadmill, trying to sweat off thirty pounds. Didn't work.

Then, I got mad at myself. What do I care what John Wall thinks of my body? He cheated on me with a woman named Stephanie.

My friend Lorraine showed me the woman's social media. She's taller than me—thinner, blonder, and she goes paddle boarding *a lot*. So many pictures of her in bikinis, and she doesn't have just the one for when she's sunning in her backyard. She has *many*. For different occasions.

John Wall cheated on me, and I sunk so low as to cyber-stalk some woman, and all he had to say to me was *We can't sell. We're underwater on the mortgage. Why don't you stay in the house?*

So I had myself a good cry in my sweat-soaked, too-tight yoga pants, and then I got in the shower.

Now I'm fussing over my hair, and trying to spackle on enough foundation that you can't tell I've been crying.

I was crazy to invite John Wall back into my life. My days are boring, but I haven't broken down in my bathroom in *years.*

I need to pull it together. The way I make meatloaf doesn't take too long, and I already washed and cut the potatoes, but I'm on a schedule. I don't want to be massaging raw meat with my bare hands when he rings the bell.

I made cake from a box before I got on the treadmill. If this goes terribly wrong, at least there'll be cake after he leaves. Right now, I'm not sure I'll be able to eat dinner. My stomach's nothing but flapping butterflies.

After I apply some mascara—no eyeshadow or lipstick, I don't want to act like this is a *thing*—I open my underwear drawer. I still have a few lacy pairs from when we were together, but they're shoved way in the back. I tug on a pair of plain pink panties and a white T-Shirt bra.

No one's gonna see them, but you feel better in decent underwear. That's the same reason I'm going to wear my favorite pale blue cashmere sweater and the jeans that make my butt look an inch higher than it rests in real life. I need as much confidence as I can get.

This is uncharted territory.

When John and I split, I thought about dating. I downloaded an app. I swiped. It only made me sad. And that pissed me off. I'd think: maybe in a few months. Once I've had a chance to go to the gym. (I didn't.) Once this class is finished. Never got around to it, though.

I haven't been alone with a man in that way in four years. But this isn't a date. There's no quid pro quo in a date. The man doesn't invite himself over.

This is more like a job. A gig. A favor. No need to get all sweaty-palmed.

I give myself a good shake and head for the kitchen, tying on my old apron that says, "Kiss the Cook." I need to remember to take it off before John gets here.

I take out the ground beef and eggs and open a can of vegetable soup. My meatloaf's really not complicated, but for some reason, I keep screwing up, dropping things. I almost add Italian seasoning instead of garlic powder. And I knock the carton of eggs on the floor. Thank the Lord none broke.

I try to focus, but the clock's getting on my nerves. I turn on some music, try to drown out the ticking, and that works for a while, but then I keep thinking I hear someone knocking at the door, and I go to check, and no one's there.

And then I forget what I'm doing.

Plus, there's sweat trickling down my back now.

And my panties are damp. For what reason, I don't know. I guess it's the sweat. I should change them, but I'll fall behind, and my goal is to plate dinner as soon as John gets here 'cause there's no way I can focus on cooking while he's in the room. Shoot, as large as he is now, I'm not sure the both of us could fit in the kitchen.

His muscles are huge, so unbelievably cut my fingers itched to touch them. Like to check if they can possibly be real. I always liked how big John was, how his shoulders worked when we made love, how his chest and arms blocked everything out. But he's at a new level now.

He could be on the cover of a men's magazine. I bet he has one of those Vs now that points between his legs.

I shake myself. My mouth's watering. Because the house smells good. That's the reason.

*Knock. Knock.*

I gush in my panties, and my cheeks burn. Oh, crap. He's here. What's wrong with me?

I wipe down the counter, tuck my hair behind my ears, and head for the door, dirty dish towel clutched in hand.

He's early. I check the clock. No, he's not. He's five minutes late. I lost track of time, daydreaming about his massive biceps.

I suck down a deep breath, but all it does is make me dizzy, so I brace myself against the entryway wall and throw open the door.

He's there. On our—my—front porch. He's even bigger than I was just imagining.

He's wearing a red flannel shirt and faded jeans. He's freshly shaven, and oh my, he smells yummy. Outdoorsy.

His lips soften, slow and tentative. His face is so fierce— cut jaw and Roman nose like a highlander or a gladiator— but there's something sweet about him when he smiles.

"Hey, Mona."

"Hi."

He holds up a bottle of wine.

"Is that a Pinot Noir?"

"Yeah. That's the kind you like, right?"

"Yeah."

He remembered. I guess it wasn't that long ago. And I did drink a lot of wine back then.

I scooch away to let him in, and he stoops and brushes a kiss across my cheek. It's quick, a split second, but the feeling lingers. His lips are cold from being outside. My face is burning hot.

I blink.

He gestures at my apron. "Kiss the cook," he says.

"Oh. Yeah." I laugh, and it's too loud; it echoes in the narrow entrance hall. "I forgot to take it off."

"Here." He gently grasps my hips and guides me to face away from him. I feel a light tug and then the strings are dangling at my side.

"I—" I hold up a hand, as if to ward him off. He's completely filling up the space, and my brain's glitching. He's so close. My nipples tighten. He doesn't miss a beat, strolling on into the living room, completely unaffected, stopping in the middle of the room.

It's like when you drive past your elementary school, and the playground seems to have magically shrunk. That's what John's doing to the living room.

I should invite him to sit. Here? Or in the dining room? We always ate every meal at the breakfast bar, but I keep my laptop and textbooks there now.

John clears his throat. "I'm sorry. I didn't get it."

"What? Oh. The ring." I sigh as I peel off my apron and fold it slowly. "I figured he pawned it. You don't have to track it down. You tried."

"He traded it. We know the guy who's got it now. Should be easy enough to get it back. It's not a problem."

I search his face. It's harder than it used to be, more angular and weathered. I don't think I'd know if he's lying anymore. Not that he ever bothered lying. *After the run, I got drunk. There was a woman. I had sex with her.*

Anxiety floods my body, makes my skin crawl.

"I'm going to check the meatloaf out and crack a window. It's too stuffy in here." I don't wait for a reply. I head for the kitchen.

I suppose I thought he'd stay put, but he follows close on my heels. It's like being stalked by a grizzly bear.

"You want a beer?" I ask, more for something to say than out of hospitality.

"Do you have a pop?"

"Sure."

I stick my head in the fridge. Oh, the cool is amazing. I've already sweated out the curls I styled with my blow dryer. Not that it matters. I shouldn't have been playing around like this is a date anyway.

The last time John Wall was in this house, he sat on that couch in the living room and confessed that he had sex with another woman. We hadn't even made love since we'd lost Lemon, and he marched in, bold as you please, and laid it out there.

I struggled more when I told my dad I dinged his car backing into a light post.

My eyes burn. Oh, no. I am not crying. Not in front of this man. No way. Of course, for me, *don't cry* is like *don't think about pink elephants.*

I slap a can into his hand, maybe a little harder than I intended.

His brow knits. "You need help?"

"I can handle it myself."

He raises his palms and eases back, propping himself on a stool at the breakfast bar. He glances at my stack of study guides.

"So, you've been taking nursing classes, eh?"

"Yup." I take the meatloaf from the oven and rest the dish on a stove burner to cool. I have the rolls ready to go, so I pop them in, and then I grab an armful of plates, utensils, napkins, salt, and pepper.

"You sure you don't need help?"

"Nope. I've got it." I sail off into the dining room. We never used it except for when we had company over. I haven't done anything but dust and vacuum in it for four years.

The rectangular farmhouse table is a hand-me-down from John's parents. They gave it to us shortly after we got married. We made love on it once to prove we could, but it was not a comfortable height, and the wood was hard as heck. I wonder if he remembers that.

Lord, now even my feet are hot. If I weren't wearing zipper-up boots, I'd kick them off and go barefoot.

I set John's place at the head, and I set mine at the opposite end. It's going to be weird, but I don't care. This whole thing is weird. What does he even want? Is this a guilt thing? Does he think if we're friendly then he doesn't have to feel bad about what he did?

And why is it so *hot* in here. I try to open the window, but I never open the dining room window, so it sticks, and I end up making myself sweatier and even more pissed off.

The timer goes off in the kitchen. Thank goodness.

I march back, ignoring where John leans on the counter all cool and casual. I snatch the rolls straight from the oven and drop them in a basket, burning my fingers.

"Hey." John grabs my wrist. "You're gonna burn yourself."

He two-steps me backwards to the sink and guides my hand under a stream of cool water. It soothes the hurt, and that just makes me madder.

"Don't manhandle me," I snap, jerking my hand back. "Go wait in the dining room. You're under foot in here."

He hesitates a second, and I don't know what I'm going to do if he refuses. I couldn't budge this man an inch if I put back into it, but eventually, he nods slowly and backs off.

I throw open the window over the sink and suck down a breath of freezing air.

That's better. I slowly become aware that my heart is racing and sweat's dripping down between my boobs. I need to calm down.

I'm over it. I've *been* over it. He made his choices. I made mine.

All I need to do is put the meatloaf and potatoes in a serving dish, microwave some green beans from a can, and finish this thing.

Before I do, I lift my sweater and flap it, letting the winter air cool my front.

A throat clears.

I whirl around, yanking the sweater down tight as I yelp. "What?!"

John grabs the wine from the counter. "If you don't mind, I was gonna open this." He's staring at my boobs. He couldn't have seen anything. I was facing the other way.

Doesn't stop him from staring, though. He always was obsessed with my boobs.

I wave him off. "Fine by me."

"You got a corkscrew?"

"You know where it is."

Oh, sheesh, I'm being so salty. I'm really not a bitch by nature. I hate that I can't control this irritation that keeps burbling up.

I wasn't even that mad when he confessed what he'd done. I was too lowdown to be truly angry. When I thought about him with that woman—Stephanie—I felt sick, not pissed. Puking, head-aching, chills and shakes *sick*.

The microwave beeps, and I shove my hands in oven mitts. I'm angry now, though. I grab the meatloaf platter, the potatoes and green beans, and the bread basket, and I schlep it into the dining room in one trip.

I plop the dishes in front of John, and I go seat myself at

the far end of the table. He poured me a glass of wine. Good. I swallow half in one gulp.

John raises an eyebrow.

"Help yourself," I say.

He waits, but when he sees I'm not moving to serve him, he takes his butter knife and cuts himself a thick slice. I forgot serving utensils. Oh, well. He's managing.

He heaps potatoes and rolls and green beans on his plate, and then he looks to me.

"Go on. I'm not hungry."

He pauses, knife and fork hovering in midair. "You sure?"

"Absolutely sure."

He shrugs, and then he tucks in. Holy moly, it's like he hasn't eaten in a week. He attacks the meat first, of course, and downs that in four bites. Then, he shovels down the potatoes. I see him looking for the butter. I forgot that, too. He can darn well get it himself if he wants it.

He must decide everything's good enough as is because he finishes the rolls in no time and helps himself to another serving of meatloaf. Well, I say serving, but he's eaten near half at this point.

Finally, he scrapes the last crumbs onto his fork, licks it clean, and his eyes drift shut. He lets out a groan of satisfaction.

"That's even better than I remember, Mona."

His lips curl up. He's content, like the cat who got the cream.

He always loved my meatloaf.

You know what?

Screw him.

He could have been eating my meatloaf this whole time if he'd kept his dick in his pants.

Or maybe that's all he missed. My cooking. Only thing worth coming back for is some Jolly Green Giant and ninety-nine cent store-brand rolls.

My eyes tickle, and I fan them, but it's too late. Hot, fat tears dribble down my cheeks. God damn it.

John blinks drowsily, and then his eyes fly wide open.

"What's wrong?" His whole body primes for action, and he scans behind him, as if he's looking for the enemy. As if it isn't him.

"Everything." It comes out a snotty, high-pitched snarl.

"What can I do?"

Now? Four years later? Screw himself. That's what he can do.

"You can put your dishes in the sink before you get the hell out of my house!"

His jaw tightens, every perfectly, overly-defined muscle he's got swells and hardens until he looks like an 80s action figure, the kind that wears a loincloth and rides tigers.

I tense. It's pure instinct. Is he going to yell back? Lose his cool? *Finally*?

I hope he yells. I dare him. I'm gonna kick his ass out the front door.

He places his hands flat on the table and cracks his neck. "I ain't leaving."

"Why not? You're good at that, making a mess and leaving. Right?"

He doesn't even pretend not to know what I'm talking about. His brow knits, like he's thinking hard, but otherwise, he's unruffled, utterly unfazed that I'm losing my mind at the foot of the table.

"Mona—" His forehead furrows deeper, a crease appearing on the bridge of his nose. "I thought I was doing the right thing by staying away."

My fists clench so tight my knuckles burn. "The right thing? The right thing is don't *fuck* another woman when you're married!"

I'm so mad that I choke on my own spit. I chug the rest of my wine to stop the hacking.

"For heaven's sake, you don't even need to file the paperwork or anything. If you wanted out to screw other women, you just had to tell me. How hard would that have been? Didn't seem hard for you walk away after the fact!"

"It was hard," he says, his voice even. Hard.

I roll my eyes. "You wanted out. You were tired of your sad-sack wife and your sad life, and you figured you'd fuck a random Stephanie, and it'd be your Get Out of Jail Free card."

"That's what you think?" He sounds genuinely surprised.

"That's what I *know*. Lorraine told me. She says *Stephanie* kept after you once we split, and you turned her down. You didn't have to have to cheat, John. You could've just said you were done with me."

"I wasn't done with you."

"Bullshit, John. You wouldn't touch me. Not for months after we lost—" I sputter, choking on my words.

"You didn't want to be touched," John says, infuriatingly calm. "You were sleeping on the sofa."

My temper blazes. "You were working double shifts. *Volunteering* for double shifts."

His gaze drifts off to the living room. I bet he wishes he could bail. Why is he even still sitting at this table? Heck, why am I?

"Go. Don't worry about it. I'll clear your place."

He sighs, scrubbing the back of his neck.

"I don't want to leave. I never wanted to leave."

He shifts his eyes to meet mine head on, and there's an intensity there I've never seen before. Shivers shoot from my nape down my spine.

"I thought leaving was for the best, but I was wrong. I wasn't strong enough for us. I know that. But I ain't making that mistake again. You can be angry, Mona. I can take it."

My blood is pounding in my ears. I don't need his permission to be angry. He's not the one who's been left wondering for years. Tormented. He knows what happened.

"I want to know." Since he's here, and so darned determined to stay, he can put some things to rest.

He draws back slightly in his chair. "Okay. What do you want to know?"

Everything. Every horrible little detail that I perseverate on when I can't sleep at night. I plunge in, irrigating the wound. "Was it a blowjob or real sex?"

"Real sex."

My shoulders hunch, but it's too late. The blow lands, and I wasn't prepared.

I always thought maybe it was just a blowjob. And then I'd tell myself a blowjob *is* real sex, and would I really feel better if it was just a blowjob? And then I'd cry and go buy a carton of ice cream up at the Speedy Grab-N-Go.

John sits there, the picture of patience, too big for the chair, almost too tall for his legs to fit under the table.

I'm going to the Grab-N-Go after this. And I'm going to buy double chocolate chunk.

"Where did you do it?"

"At the clubhouse."

"Where in the clubhouse?"

He looks up at the ceiling. Answer's not there, dude. "I don't know, Mona. A storage room. In the back."

"How?"

"*How?*"

"What *position?*"

"Uh. She was, uh, bent over some boxes."

"Did you kiss her?"

"Yes."

I bite down on the inside of my cheek so hard I taste copper. "Did you wear a condom?"

"Yes."

"You had a condom? You brought condoms with you to the clubhouse?"

"She had one. She came on to me."

"So, you had to say yes? You slipped, and oops, your dick fell in her?"

"I didn't say that."

"Did she come on to you before?"

Quiet. The clock ticks. The neighbor's dog barks.

"Yeah."

"You never mentioned it."

He shakes his head. "You were so torn up about—"

I raise my hand.

"Stop."

My heart's thudding in my chest. I can't breathe, but that's crazy. This is *not* hurting as bad as I feel like it is. I'm fine. It happened a long time ago.

But my body thinks it's happening now. Like every time I get my period, and I see the first red smear on the toilet paper, and I panic, even though there's no reason.

"I wasn't 'torn up.' I was *grieving.*"

He closes his eyes. Like maybe I landed a blow that time.

"Why?" I ask. "Why did you do it?"

He's silent again, and it's painful, mocking. I'm a noisy, sobbing mess, and he's a statue.

"*Why?*"

"Anything I say is gonna make you feel worse."

"I deserve to know!"

He pushes up from the table, hands fisted, legs braced. "Goddamn it, Mona, I ain't sayin' nothin' that's gonna make you cry any more!"

"You...you...asshole!" My forearm flies across the table, sending the plate crashing into the wall. The wine glass falls to the floor, shattering on impact.

I stare down at the mess. John stares at me.

I drop to my knees.

"Wait!" he barks, but he's too late. I land right on a shard of glass, sharp enough to pierce the denim of my jeans. I cry out in pain.

"Don't move!" He lunges for me.

Ow, ow, ow. How big a shard did I land on? I swear, I can feel it scraping against my patella.

I raise my arms to grab the table and hoist myself up, but instead, there's John, lifting me, cradling me against his massive chest, and my arms wind around his neck.

"Stay still, baby. We'll check it out. It'll be okay."

There's blood blossoming through my jeans, the sliver of glass sticking out. Oh, gross. My head swims.

I'm fine around other people's bodily fluids, but my own...it's not good.

John sets me on the kitchen counter next to the sink. He raises my chin with a nudge of his knuckle. "Don't look. You'll throw up."

He snags the first aid kit from the corner cabinet, and then he washes his hands. "I'll take the glass out, and then we'll see if you need to go to the hospital."

"I don't need to go to the hospital. I can fix myself up." I say it, but I don't know if push came to shove that I could give myself stitches. I'd need another glass of wine first, definitely.

John doesn't argue. He ignores me, rummaging through the first aid kit until he finds a gauze pad.

"Okay. Are you ready?" His deep brown eyes meet mine. He's so wide, he fills up my entire field of vision. All I can smell is his soap, and all I can see is his broad chest. His flannel shirt seems like it's really soft.

"Okay." He plucks out the glass, so quickly there's only an instant of pain, and then he immediately applies pressure with the gauze to my knee. "We need to get you out of these pants."

"Not the first time I've heard that." I know it's not the time and place, but I'm overwhelmed, and a tad tipsy, and the cut hurts like a son of a gun.

John briefly presses his forehead to mine, and his lips curve.

"We'll give it a minute or so to staunch the bleeding."

"I need to clean up that mess." I can't believe I did that. I am not the dramatic *Housewives* type at all.

John takes my hand, and replaces his with mine. "Keep up the pressure. I'll go clean up the wine."

"It's my mess."

"Not really." He flashes me a rueful half-smile, and then he heads to the pantry for the cleaning supplies.

I guess I still keep everything in the same place as when we lived here together. Why wouldn't I? People keep mops in the pantry and first aid kits in awkwardly-shaped cabinets. Everyone keeps a corkscrew in the junk drawer.

It's unsettling, though. It's been four years, and he can move through this house like he hasn't been gone a day.

Why didn't I redecorate? Or reorganize, at least? I never had the money to move. Our mortgage is insanely low; we must have bought at the bottom of the market. But shouldn't I have made the place my own?

I did take down our wedding picture. It's in a box in the garage.

It doesn't take John that long to clean up. He brings his dirty dishes in when he comes back. I checked the gauze a few times, and the bleeding's slowed down.

"Ready to take your pants off?"

"If you can help me down, I can do it myself. You can see yourself out."

He snorts. "I haven't had dessert. I was promised chocolate cake."

Tiredness, like a lead blanket, rolls down over me. It's not blood loss. It's centered too much in my hollow chest. "John." His eyes find mine like magnets. "I don't get what's going on here."

"I'm fixing shit." His jaw firms. Then, he gathers me in his arms again and heads for the bedroom, snagging the first aid kit as he goes. I don't have time to reply. He moves so suddenly for such a huge man.

"I'm going to lay you on the bed to take your pants off. Then I'm going to help you to the bathroom, disinfect the wound, and if I ain't mistaken, I'm gonna have to apply a butterfly closure or two. We can eat cake after."

"I can take my own pants off."

"I can handle it myself." He does a terrible, squeaky impression of me from earlier as he places me carefully on the bed, tugs off my shoes, and then—as I'm halfheartedly swatting at him—he pops a button, unzips me, and gently eases my jeans down from the ankles.

"John!" I shriek, and then my eyes catch on the zipper of his jeans, and I freeze.

He's got a boner. A *huge* one. He's keeping his eyes above

my waist, but they're still dazed and dark-chocolate brown, like they used to get when he got excited.

I used to drive him wild. It was crazy. I'd bend over to straighten up the magazines on the coffee table, or we'd be hanging out at the pool in the summer, and he'd start staring, and his eyes would get deadly serious and swirly, and then he'd come at me like a starving beast.

That was before the babies. A long time ago.

"What are you doing?" I ask, warily. He offers me a hand.

"Helping you to the bathroom. Is there antiseptic in the medicine cabinet?"

"There's some peroxide."

"That'll do." He helps me stand, and he bears my weight while I hop to the en suite. I prop myself on the edge of the tub, and he grabs some cotton balls from the jar on the shelf above the toilet.

I screw up the courage to look at my knee. It's bloody, and it definitely needs to be bandaged, but I don't think it needs stitches. My cheeks heat. That was a really stupid thing to do.

I clear my throat. "I'm sorry about that. I lost my temper."

John glances at me. His shoulders go almost wall-to-wall, and he had to duck his head to come in the door. I couldn't get past him if I wanted to.

"Fair enough." He kneels in front of me, and dabs my knee with a cold, wet cotton ball. It fizzes. "You can take it out on me, you know. Instead of the china."

"I've never hit a person in my life."

"I know. Might make you feel better. I can take a punch."

I suck in a breath as he hits a raw spot. He instantly stops and blows on my knee. It's not hygienic, but it does ease the hurt.

"What if I knocked you out?" I babble on. "You'd put a hole in my floor."

"We could take it outside."

"The neighbors would call the police."

"Mr. and Mrs. Chaudhry? They'd place bets."

"They'd bet on me," I brag.

John's applying the bandages now, and the sting is ebbing. The teasing comes so naturally. It makes me sad—it feels familiar as home.

"Of course, they would. The odds would not be in my favor," John says, finishing with the bandage. He leaves his hand on my leg. His thumb strokes the inside of my thigh, almost behind my knee. Little shivers follow his touch.

"But you'd fight me anyway?" I should push his hand away, but I don't. It's nice. Not too ticklish. My belly stirs with flutters. Nice. Nervous, but nice.

"I would fight for you," he says.

"I don't believe you," I whisper. We've both lowered our voices.

"I left without a fight last time. I ain't gonna do that again."

I drop my head, stare at the white and black tile. "Why did you stay away, then, if you didn't want to go?"

I can't bear to look at him while he answers. It takes him a minute.

"I told myself I stayed away 'cause you asked. And doin' what you asked was the least I could do after I fucked up so bad. But then, after a time, I came to understand that I was full of shit."

He pauses. I wait, steeled for words to rip me apart where my scars are barely mended.

"I was punishing myself. For hurting you. For letting you down. For being *weak*." He sighs, and it's a beatdown kind of sound. "And I was ashamed of myself. Simple as that, really."

He reaches for a washcloth, and turns on the faucet. "Shame's a powerful thing."

I don't know what to say.

He takes the warm washrag, and gently wipes away a streak of blood that dried on my calf. The cloth is rough against my skin, but his touch is so careful.

"You want an aspirin?" His voice has dropped an octave. He's so close, I can see the stubble on his chin.

"No. I'm good."

My brain's all muzzy, piecing together what he said, matching it with how I feel. The man I knew. This man kneeling on one knee in front of me, taking up an entire bathroom, more intent on my leg than anyone's ever been on any part of me.

I think he wants me. Again. Still?

It hurts too bad, so I don't often let myself think all the way back to the beginning. I was in high school. I'd had a boyfriend, but he was crap in bed. No offense to him. He didn't have much experience, either, but he had way more than I did, so I sort of thought the way he did it was the way it was done.

John didn't try anything with me until I turned eighteen. Just sometimes, he'd bail, out of the blue. We'd be hanging out in my parents' basement—they didn't much care what I did as long as I didn't make a racket—and he'd say, "Er. Goodnight." And he'd be gone.

And then for my eighteenth birthday, he took me to a fancy restaurant in Pyle. It overlooked the river, and the waiter talked for a good five minutes about where the fish was sourced and how long the filet was aged.

Then he took me for a walk along the Luckahannock,

and he gave me the diamond ring we'd picked out together a few weeks before. He'd wrapped the box; did a real terrible job. I had laughed. He'd slipped the ring on my finger and said, "Haven't changed your mind, have you?"

I said no, and I swear, it was like he heard a starter pistol in his head. We were in a cab, then at the hotel, and then his face was buried between my legs in no less than ten minutes flat. I couldn't keep up, but it didn't matter because everything felt so, so good. He wasn't checking boxes until he could score for himself. He was going to *town*.

My face is flaming hot thinking about it.

John's kneeling on the bathroom floor, patient as can be, his hand wrapped lightly around my left calf. He's shifted back so he's resting on his heels. There's a question in his eyes.

I can see his pants now. They're definitely tented.

I ease my thighs apart just a little. Not on purpose. Not really. His gaze drops instantly. A grunt, almost a pant, escapes from his lips.

It probably doesn't mean anything. He's a red-blooded man. I'm in my underwear. I could be anyone. *Stephanie.* Anyone.

I go to press my legs back together, but he's so fast, his hand slides up from my calf to my uninjured knee in a split second. He's not applying much pressure, but he's bracing my thigh right where it is.

His breath comes quicker. "Don't stop, baby. Let me see a little more."

I shouldn't. He's intent on the crotch of my panties. There are little tufts of hair spilling past the elastic. It didn't occur to me to shave—'cause I would never in a million, zillion years be flashing John Wall my cooch, right?—and I've never had the money or the gumption to wax. So, it's clear I've got a bush, and the gusset is damp. He can see it all.

His nose twitches.

And smell. Oh, what am I doing?

I'm turning him on. I think.

He urges me to open up with the lightest pressure. I let him widen me up. His gaze flies up to my face, as if he's checking I'm really okay. Like he can't believe this is happening. That hungry look is there, but he's restraining himself with an iron control he never had before.

Maybe because he's older now. Thirty-two.

Maybe because I'm older now, and not nearly as thin and cute. There's an obvious belly pouching out of my panties, and I don't do highlights or manicures anymore.

I tighten my grip on the tub, and my palms slip. They're sweaty.

"Let me see, baby."

His hand's still resting on my good knee, but he's looking at my boobs now. He moves, gently stroking the top of my thighs down to my calves, careful to avoid the bandaged cut.

"Take the sweater off for me."

I couldn't do that. But his eyes are darkening. He licks his lips, and he shifts forward. Now his knees are between my ankles, spreading my stance even wider. My pussy lips part with a wet pop, and more cream drips into my panties.

I'm getting soaked.

"Come on." His voice is deep and gentle, calm and demanding. He takes my hand and places it to the hem of my sweater. "Show me, baby."

I knead the faux cashmere in my fingers. I love this sweater. It's soft and machine washable.

Almost without thinking, I fist the hem and pull it over my head like some bold woman from a movie. Static electrifies strands of my hair. I drop the sweater in the tub and try desperately to smooth my hair back into place, much good it does.

I glance down. My boobs are heavy, puffing over the cups. I have very dark areolas, and my nipples themselves are pretty big when they get hard. There's plenty visible through my bra.

John's devouring my boobs with his eyes. He shifts as close as he can get; his knees meet the side of the tub, forcing my knees wider, as wide as they can go, spreading my pussy lips until I gape. He wraps his arms around my waist, and strokes the small of my back. There's only inches between us. I feel so small, so naked.

Shivers dance across my exposed skin. I've never been this close to a man this muscular before. When we were together, John was a big man, but I'd call him beefy, not jacked. This man is *shredded*.

This man could be with any woman. He probably has. Oh, crap.

"Do you have a girlfriend?"

He blinks, his hand suspended in the air between us. He was aiming to cop a feel. He fists, then lowers, the questing hand.

"No."

"Don't you want to know if I have a boyfriend?"

"You don't."

"How do you know?"

"I know." There's no doubt in his voice. Does he think I couldn't get a man if I wanted one? I've been asked out a few times. Given, twice was at the Grab-and-Go at a dubious hour of night, and once was a friend of Lorraine's that I'm positive she put up to it, but still. They count.

John traces my frown with a calloused finger. "Do you

want me to be jealous? Do you wanna know that the thought of you with another man drives me fucking insane? It does. You wanna hurt me, destroy me, you got that power. I know it ain't fair. It's hypocritical as hell, but if you let any other man touch this body, it'd kill me."

Huh. How'd he even know if I had a boyfriend? How would I know if he has a girlfriend?

"Are you with anyone?"

"No."

"Are you sleeping with anyone right now?"

"No."

I shiver. Fold my arms tight, squishing my aching boobs. John clenches his jaw so tightly the tic on his forehead starts pulsing.

Then he pulls his phone out of his back pocket.

"Here." He grabs my hand, giving me the phone. "10-12."

"That's our anniversary."

"I know."

I hold the phone, staring at it stupidly.

"Go on. Check my messages and shit. I ain't with no one else."

"I don't need to check your phone."

He takes the phone back, taps a few times, and then holds it up. It's his chat history.

"Is that a picture of a coyote?"

His lip twitches up. "Turns out, yeah. It is."

"You don't need to show me your phone."

He sniffs, and then he tucks it away. He falls quiet. I think about how I can gracefully retrieve my sweater from the tub.

Finally, after what feels like forever, he says, "I miss your humming."

What?

"I miss how you hum movie music when you fold laundry."

That is a habit of mine. I don't know classical music, but when you hum, you want something with no words. So... movie scores.

"I miss texting you where I'm at, and you sending me pictures of cats and shit."

Memes. He's talking about memes.

"I miss your cooking, and I miss how you laugh, and I miss these fucking beautiful tits, and I always said if I got the chance, I'd tell you."

"That I have beautiful tits?"

"Hell yeah. Beautiful everything."

"I'm not as fit as when we were together. I'm not all ripped like you."

"More cushion for the pushin'."

"You did *not* just say that." I can't help but snicker. His dad always said that about his mom. She'd slap him and then shimmy her butt around the kitchen. My smile falls. I miss John Senior and Kelly. They make a point to call and check in, but it's not the same.

"They miss you, too, you know." He always could read my mind.

"Are we really talking about your parents while I'm topless in the bathroom?"

"We're gonna talk about whatever for as long as you need. You need to ask me somethin', ask."

"What did she have that I didn't have? It was 'cause she was happy. Wasn't it? 'Cause she wasn't all defective?"

My skin puckers with goosebumps. All of a sudden, I'm so cold.

John's eyes fade, his clenched jaw becomes a grimace. "It was because I was weak."

He rubs his rough hands up and down my arms, as if he's trying to warm me up. "You needed me. I didn't know what to do. I couldn't help. Couldn't even get out of your way. You told me you needed space, and I didn't listen."

"I said I needed space?" I don't remember that, but it's kind of ringing a vague bell.

"Yeah. Like encouraging me to go out. And I stuck at home, and you got mad. You needed to be alone, and I didn't give you that."

"I was a mess." That's somewhat of an understatement.

"You were mine. Best thing that ever happened to me. To this day." His brown eyes are shining. His touch has lightened, gentled.

"To this day?"

"Baby, I been waitin' for some punk to steal an old lady's ring for four damn years."

He's funning. I don't believe him. Obviously.

His eyes search my face, and it's like he reads something there. He eases back onto his heels.

"You're not sure," he says.

How can I be?

"Did I tell you we got the name of the guy who bought the ring off Tommy?"

"You did?" The conversation's changed so quickly— again—that I'm struggling to keep up. Besides, my body's urging me to close the space between us.

"Yeah. I'm gonna go see if he's still got it."

"I'm sure it's a wild goose chase."

"Maybe so. I'm still gonna go after it. But I want something in return."

My lower belly clenches. "What?"

"I want to take you out."

I must look as befuddled as I feel.

"On a date," he clarifies. "We get dressed up. I pick you up at seven."

"John, you don't have to do this." I'm starting to feel self-conscious. I go to cross my arms, but he grabs my hands. Raises them to his lips. Brushes kisses across my knuckles.

"I don't want you to get me wrong. I want your pussy. So bad, baby, it fuckin' hurts. But I don't want to break anything 'cause I put more strain on it before it's ready. I want to buy you a steak, Mona Wall. I want to hear about your day. I want you to blow your hair into curls again for me, and wear those fancy shoes with the heels that you keep in the box."

"I lent them to Lorraine, and she didn't give them back."

"Then go barefoot. Just say yes."

This is crazy. It's all crazy.

John squeezes my hands.

"Okay," I say.

He flashes me the biggest, brightest smile. And then he rises to his feet, helps me up, and guides me to the bed.

I perch on the edge, and he drops a kiss on my forehead.

"Remember how we'd be makin' out in your basement, and I'd get up all of a sudden and bail?"

I nod, my lips curling up.

"'Cause I knew if I stayed another second, I wouldn't be able to stop myself from burying my cock in your pussy."

My face flames. John always did have a mouth on him.

"I'm gonna see myself out now, baby. But I'm gonna be back tomorrow with a ring."

He turns to leave but he stops in the doorway, filling it with his broad shoulders. "And so we're clear. This ain't me leaving."

"It's not?"

"Nope. 'Cause I guess you don't know this, but my heart's

right there." He nods to where I sit on the bed. "Has been since I first laid eyes on you."

My chest floods with warmth, and worry follows closely behind. I fidget, fiddle with the comforter, plucking a loose thread.

John never used to say things like this. "Love you, babe" was pretty much the extent of his sweet-talk. I don't know what to make of all this.

"I'm lockin' the door after me, and I'm closing that window over the kitchen sink. You don't keep that unlocked at night, do you?"

Now that sounds more like the John Wall I knew.

"I do. Made a blinking arrow and a sign that says *Thieves, Enter Here* out of Christmas lights, too. You'll see it if you go out the back door."

"Smartass."

"Worrywart."

"You'll be ready when I come for you tomorrow night, won't you, Mona?"

Ready?

My heart's been pummeled, my mind's whirling, and my body's thrumming with excitement and occasional misfiring sparks of insecurity and rage. Ready? No.

"I'll be dressed," I say.

We've come this far.

It'd be a shame to throw in the towel before Miss Janice gets her ring.

## 6

## WALL

I know as soon as I leave, Mona's gonna get all up in her head, so I give her a wave, tell her I'm goin' to get her ring, and to be ready by seven.

I call Heavy on my way to my ride. He's awake, clackin' away on his computer. The man is a machine.

"Did Forty tell you about Ethan Eckels?"

"He did."

"There a plan?"

"Yup. We're gonna ride out at four. Get him while he's still in bed. You at Mona's?"

"I was."

"We can handle this if you need to be somewhere else."

"I'll be there by four."

I drive off, and then I circle back, turning off my headlights before I get to our house.

Our house. She ain't changed nothin'. Took some pictures down, but other than that, it's like the day she kicked me out. That's got to mean something, right?

I park in front of the Chaudry's and watch as one-by-one, she turns the lights out. The living room. The dining room. The bedroom.

More than anything, I wanted to stay. She wasn't indifferent. I saw the wet spot on her panties. Saw her nipples pokin' through her bra. Mona ain't wild. She don't cuss much or party. But she loves to fuck. I could've got her there.

But then what when she wakes up still mad? I mean, she damn near flipped the table. She got cause. I ain't doubting that. And maybe pissed off is better than broken. I do know adding sex to the equation ain't gonna make things simpler. This is too important. I gotta play it slow.

I watch our house, dozing off in the frigid cab of my truck, until it gets close to go time, and I head off toward Petty's Mill. Guess I'm gonna go fuck up a drug dealer at the ass-crack of dawn on a Saturday morning.

I knew Heavy would want to deal with this quickly once he learned Eckels is still in the area. I shouldn't be surprised that he's ready to tackle it first thing. The man runs a multi-million-dollar construction company, full custom garage, strip club, and quasi-legal motorcycle club. He's efficient by nature.

When I pull up to the clubhouse, there's a windowless white van parked out front with the back doors open.

"Wall! Get in here so we's can go! Smells like ass in here!" That's Creech. He's probably not sober, and definitely the source of the ass smell.

"I'm here." I hoist myself into the back. It's jam-packed with brothers. Heavy's in the passenger seat, and the prospect with the straggly beard, Mikey, is driving.

The rest of us squat on overturned Steel Bones Construction buckets. Forty, Charge, Nickel, and Grinder along one side. Pig Iron, Creech, me, and an older dude in khaki pants and a pale-blue collared shirt along the other.

One of these things is *not* like the others.

"Who's the civilian?" I mutter to Creech.

"Hell if I know. I was passed out in the commons, and I heard 'Who wants to go fuck someone up?' so I came along. You got a smoke?"

I shake my head. I don't—I quit when Mona was expecting Peanut—but I'm hoping someone does. Anything would smell better than unwashed Creech after a hard night of what had to have been wrestling pigs in shit.

Creech turns to Grinder, and the old man spares him the cigarette he keeps tucked behind his ear. The van fills with smoke, and the civilian fails to stifle a cough.

I look to Forty. He's ex-military, so he tends to run our operations. One thing I like about Steel Bones is everybody's got a role. Steel and Smoke was a social club. Besides road captain, and the dude who handled dues, there wasn't much in the way of organization. Steel Bones is a well-oiled machine.

Heavy's the brains. The shot caller. Forty's his right-hand. Nickel's an enforcer, and he's insane. Never seen a man fight with less provocation or concern for his bones and soft tissue. Charge is the pretty boy. The hillbilly charmer. He smooths things out when possible, and takes the rap when it's not.

Pig Iron's the treasurer, and Creech does ink and piercings. I'm muscle. We're a motley crew, our only real connections the cut and the ink on our skin. But we're family.

The dude in the collared shirt, though. I ain't seen him around before.

I finally catch Forty's eye and raise an eyebrow.

"Oh, yeah. That's Mr. Smith," Forty says.

Sounds like an alias. Of course, there are also thousands of Mr. Smiths in western PA.

"Mr. Smith lost his daughter last year to a fentanyl overdose. He and his wife are raising their granddaughter. How old is she?"

He clears his throat and swipes his palms on his thighs. "Four. Hailey is four. Almost five."

I begin to connect the dots. "Nice to meet you, Mr. Smith."

He nods. Dude's face is white as a ghost. He's freshly shaven with a businessman's haircut. He's wearing loafers, but I've seen that look in a man's eyes before. I hope no one gave him a gun.

"We get the ring first, yes?" I ask Forty.

"Affirmative."

The rest of the drive is silent except for Grinder hawking loogies and Creech babbling at some woman on his cell phone. When we pull up in front of a Victorian that's seen much better days, Forty barks, "Cuts."

We shrug them off and pass them up to the prospect for safekeeping. Then, Forty passes around the ski masks. I tie on a blue bandana. Ski masks make my face itch.

Mr. Smith eyeballs his mask like he don't quite know what to do with it.

"Goes over your head," Creech quips.

Mr. Smith smiles wryly and squares his shoulders.

"You ready for this?" Forty asks him. Mr. Smith nods. "All right, then. Charge and Creech, go right. Grinder and Pig Iron, go left. Wall, you got the door."

"Yup." I always get the door.

"On three. One—" Forty holds up his fist, every inch the ex-Army Ranger.

But we ain't exactly disciplined, and we love to fuck with him.

A half dozen men bust out of the back of the van, Creech

racing hellbent for leather with a lit cigarette dangling from his lips, Nickel elbowing past me to the door and kicking it open in three wild kicks.

The living room is clear. Nickel races up the stairs, and there's a ruckus at the back. The intel was good. Eckels has set himself up in business again. There's CCTV, an alarm system, which might explain the action at the back. He had a few seconds head start.

"Get your hands off me, you asshole! Ethan!"

"I ain't touching you!" Nickel's urging a woman down the stairs, and he speaks the truth. He's not laying a finger on her, just crowding her, but no one wants a man with eyes that crazy too close to their back.

The woman is a piece of work. Huge hair, blonde dye job with inch-long roots, pinched face. She's wearing a clean T-shirt and panties, and compulsively scratching her forearms. I saw a lot of women like her when I was firefighting. She's holding it together, barely, but the bill's gonna come due soon.

"Where's Ethan Eckels?" Forty demands. He's managed to catch up with us.

"Who?" The woman folds her arms, shooting daggers at all of us. She has a ring on her finger. Diamond with blue sapphires and a gold band.

"Give me that ring," I bark.

"Fuck you." She tucks her hand in the crook of her arm to hide the ring. "Ethan! ETHAN!"

As if on cue, Creech and Charge muscle a shirtless guy with a faux hawk into the room. Pig Iron follows with a piece dangling in his hand. Looks like a .45 revolver. What, does this guy rob stagecoaches?

"He pull on you?" Forty asks our boys. This goes down real, real ugly if he did.

"Nope. The dumbass was climbing down the trellis. He threw the gun down first. I just picked it up." Pig Iron snorts.

The guy's wearing nothing but baggy gym shorts. Guess pitching it wasn't the dumbest move?

"If this is a robbery, you better know, we have a security system. The cops are already on the way. You better—"

"Shut up, Brianna." Eckels glares at the woman.

"Ethan—" she hisses back.

"Shut. Up."

"First smart thing you've done." The gravelly voice comes from behind, and we all shift, allowing Heavy into the room. He has the civilian at his side.

Eckels tries to back up, but he hits Charge's chest. Charge bumps him forward.

If you don't know Heavy, he is a man who can make you piss your pants. When shit gets real, he don't seem entirely human. More like a cross between an orc and the devil. And the lead guitarist from an 80s metal band.

Part of it's his voice. It can go so deep, it don't sound natural. Part of it's the way he looks at people who ain't Steel Bones. Like they're ants. Or air.

Brianna shuts up.

"You have a ring?" He opens his hand. She tugs it off, dashes forward to drop it in his palm, and then scampers back to Nickel. Guess she's figured he's the lesser of two evils.

Heavy passes me the ring, and I tuck it in my pocket. I feel a little better. Like I got something going for me now. Money in the bank.

"Brianna, do you have people somewhere who care about you?" Heavy uses that tone, the one that makes any room echo like church.

She's crying now, soundlessly. I don't like to see a woman

cry, and I don't get off on frightening one, neither. But I've known these men many years. They ain't gonna hurt her.

"Parents? Grandparent?" Heavy bores into her with his black eyes.

She sniffles, staring at the floor. "Yeah. I guess so."

"You should go visit them. Bet it's been awhile since you've seen them, yeah?"

She ponders this a minute.

"Ethan?" She looks to her man.

He shrugs, doesn't even spare her a glance. "Whatever, Brianna. Don't ask me."

"Can I get my things?" She asks Heavy.

He jerks his chin toward the stairs. She races up them, and comes back with pants on, a purse, and a cell phone tucked in her bra. Forty grabs the phone, and fishes for her wallet. Looking for ID.

"Prospect!" Heavy calls over his shoulder. Mikey jogs forward, and Grinder rotates to his lookout position at the front blinds. "Walk Brianna—"

He looks at Forty.

"Anne Devers of Pyle," Forty supplies.

"Walk Brianna Anne Devers to the nearest convenience store, and call her folks to pick her up. Wait with her until they come. Get their tag number."

"Yes, sir." The prospect crooks his elbow and offers it to Brianna. She ignores it.

"Are you gonna kill him?" She asks in a whisper, her arms clutching her purse so tightly her knuckles are swollen and white.

"Do you really want to ask me that?" Heavy meets her wild eyes, and she swallows.

"That's my engagement ring."

Heavy has this strange effect on people. Mesmerizing

fear and then a kind of hypnotism. I've seen many men confess to him, drunk and sober. It's an oddity, for sure.

"It was stolen."

She drops her head. "It figures."

"You knew."

"I guess I did." Her voice is almost inaudible.

The prospect offers his arm, again. She sighs and heads out the front door on her own steam. We wait until Pig Iron manages to wrestle the busted front door back into its frame before we deal with our remaining issue.

Forty marches over to loom over our drug-dealing friend. "We told you to get gone, Eckels."

"I ain't in Petty's Mill." He still has some fight left in him.

"What was it I said?" Heavy looks to Forty.

"You suggested he drive 'til he hits water, and then he could stop. Or keep going. You left that open."

"I hear California and Florida are both good places for a fresh start," Pig Iron muses.

"Turn over a new leaf." Creech plops himself on a very nice leather couch which doesn't match the peeling walls or the moth-eaten rug.

"Good places to find yourself." Heavy adds, stepping forward. "Yet, we find you here. In the next town over."

"I ain't affecting your business." Eckels' eyes are darting around the room like a lizard. He's lookin' for an out, but there isn't one. He's surrounded. So he tries wheedling. "In a way, I'm a benefit. Law's always looking at me. Don't have time to look at anyone else."

Well, that was the wrong thing to say.

To the outside eye, Steel Bones is one hundred percent legit. We have an excellent relationship with local law enforcement. I myself have organized charity rides with the local chapter of the Blue Hawks.

Eckels is suggesting he knows something different. The chances of him walking out of this house have decreased exponentially.

Heavy doesn't respond for a minute. Then he says, "I want to introduce you to someone. Everett?"

Yeah, we're using names now. Eckels ain't gonna be breathing much longer.

The civilian steps forward.

"You want to take your mask off, so he can look you in the eye?" Heavy asks.

Mr. Smith does. There's pure hate and rage on the man's face.

"Do you want to say anything?" Heavy asks. The man's Adam apple bobs but no sound comes out. He's past words. Heavy turns to Eckels. "You might remember his daughter. Serena Smith. I think you gave her a ring, too."

"You got her hooked on that— that— *garbage*. You killed her. Her mother— We—" Smith's face, even his scalp where his hair is thinning, is bright red. Spit flies as he speaks.

Smith looks to Heavy. He has to crane his neck.

"Whenever you're ready, friend."

And Smith jumps Eckels. He's so quick, Charge and Nickel almost don't manage to pin Eckels' arms back in time.

It's clear Smith has never thrown a punch before, but damn, his heart's in it. He aims for the face, sending Charge and Nickel bobbing and ducking his wild swings. He cracks Eckel's nose and jaw. Blood splatters. Charge and Nickel leap back to avoid the spray, and I move to step in, but Eckels is down.

He's screaming, and Smith is driving his brown loafers into Eckels' unprotected ribs as he desperately tries to protect his mashed face.

Smith is screaming, too, a wordless wailing that spears me in the guts. I don't know his loss, but the sound of his cries aren't foreign to me. Grief is grief.

I find my eyes are prickling as I watch Smith's energy ebb and the tears streak down his cheeks.

Finally, he stands still over Eckels' writhing, bloody body, his fists still clenched in rage.

"My Serena was a *good* girl. We loved her." His voice breaks. "He stole her away from us. Turned her into—" He can't bring himself to say the words. "She was a good girl. She was *happy*, and we loved her, goddamn it!"

He meets each of our eyes, demanding we understand, that we acknowledge his love and his loss. My brothers aren't cowards. They hold his gaze. But they don't understand. None of them except maybe Pig Iron.

I step forward, rest my arm around his heaving shoulders. "She was your little girl."

A ragged sob rips from his throat. "He killed her."

"You loved her."

"I would have done *anything* for her."

"I know." As I lead him outside, I untie my bandana and hand it to him. He wipes speckles of blood from his face.

The street is as quiet as it was when we pulled up. While we were inside, a prospect showed up in the truck that we use for transferring sensitive cargo.

I help Mr. Smith into the van. He's totally out of it.

"Did I kill him?" he asks.

"Nope."

"But I hurt him."

"Yup."

"Is he gonna die?"

I shrug. "We all do, eventually."

"I hope it hurts. I hope he feels it." A small spark flares in his eyes. "Do you have kids?"

The muscles in my stomach tense against the question. "Ah, no. My wife and I...we had some losses."

"I'm sorry." He pats my knee.

We both fall silent and sag back against the metal walls. It's uncomfortable as hell, but I don't think either of us has much energy left.

That's the first time I ever said that to someone. About the babies.

I had to tell my ma—three times—but it was on the phone. She was the one who told my dad and the rest of the family. Ma was really worried about Mona; she fussed a lot about what she could do to help her, but there wasn't anything. Mona either wanted to pretend nothing happened, or she wanted to be left alone.

With Peanut, Mona told the people she'd confided in about the pregnancy, and they offered condolences when they saw me, but we kept the news quieter for Jellybean and Lemon, so it didn't ever come up.

Lemon was the hardest. Mona had started to show. She hid it with big shirts and layers. She thought it'd been unlucky that she told people about Peanut, so she was being really quiet about it. When we lost the baby, except for Ma and the obstetrician, there was no one to tell.

It's a hard feeling. That you've lost something, and the world continues on as if it doesn't matter. You gotta go to work, gear up, go out on calls, eat dinner, shoot the shit, as if everything is exactly the same as it ever was.

The only time you hear their nicknames anymore is in your head. And you can't talk about it with your wife. You can't add to her burden.

I exhale and shift on the bucket, try to rearrange my bulk before the other brothers join us.

"Serena is a pretty name," I say.

"She was the prettiest little girl. The best kid." Mr. Smith offers me a wavering smile. "Hailey is her spitting image."

I smile back. "You need another bandana for those knuckles?"

He's resting his hands gingerly on his lap. They're bloody and swelling like hell. He's definitely broken some bones. "It would be appreciated."

I give him the extra I keep in my back pocket.

We sit there, waiting for the others. I slide my hand into my pocket and slip the ring on my little finger.

Mission accomplished.

## 7

## MONA

There's no lying to myself this time. It's a date.

John texted at six o'clock in the morning that he got the ring. He texted an hour later asking if Broyce's was okay for dinner.

Despite the fancy places they've opened up on the downtown waterfront, Broyce's is still the most popular restaurant in Petty's Mill. It's a dive, but the steaks and hush-puppies are the best in the state. I told him Broyce's was fine.

Then he called around noon and asked me if I'd rather drive into Pyle. Go someplace fancy. He sounded nervous on the phone. If I didn't know him, I wouldn't have been able to tell. When he's nervous, his voice drops an octave, and he boils his sentences down to subject and verb.

Not that he's the nervous type. Only ever around me.

A flush of heat creeps up my chest as I step out of the shower. It's only four in the afternoon, but I wanted to give myself lots of time to get ready in case I get all sweaty again.

I can't believe I'm getting ready for a date with John Wall. Or that I'm excited.

There's a thrum in my belly, and I've got that first date energy. Music's blaring from my phone, and I'm swaying my hips as I apply my eyeshadow, using all three colors like they show in the diagram on the back of the box. Usually, I swipe on a nude and call it a day.

These days, I don't spend much time getting ready, but it's funny how it comes back to you like riding a bike. Batting your eyelashes against a tissue to get off the excess mascara. Dabbing scent behind your knees and ears.

I don't think I've used my perfume since John left. It doesn't go bad, though, does it?

I squint in the mirror at the finished product. It's the middle of winter, so my hair's lank and dark, but at least there aren't strands sticking up from static. My face is round and my nose is pointy. I look like a 3D animated character. But a cute one.

With my makeup done, I can even pass for pretty. I didn't think so when I was younger—my mom's voice was too loud in my head—but I've got my charms.

Mom was big on advice. Pull your shoulders back and no one will notice that flabby gut. Smile with your lips closed to hide those horse teeth.

I flash a smile at the mirror. It's a nice smile, big and bright. Happy looks good on me.

I return to the bedroom, ignoring the outfit I'd laid out on the bed, a conservative black button up shirt and gray pants. Job interview clothes. I pull out a sweater in dusty-rose that's cut a little too tight and my second favorite jeans. They're worn with a hole or two, but they do magical things for my butt.

I check myself again in the full-length mirror. You can see all my curves. I suck them in and let 'em out. Then, I draw my shoulders back. John's gonna stare at my boobs all night long.

My lips curve up as I tug on snow boots and go wait in the living room. I'm ready two hours early. Well, crap.

There's a small hole in the wrist of my sweater. Maybe I should change. Maybe it's a touch too clingy. I get up, and the doorbell rings.

Who could it be? It's five o'clock on a Saturday. I'm not expecting any packages.

I go to the door and stick an eye to the peephole.

And there's John, hands jammed in his thick Carhartt jacket, his breath visible in the air. He's stamping snow off his boots.

Why does he have snow on his boots? The walk and porch are shoveled.

And why's he here so early? Is he canceling? Maybe something came up, and he's come to just drop off the ring.

That's okay. I'd be fine.

I steel myself and open the door. He smiles, wide and blinding.

"Oh, good, you're ready. We can beat the rush."

I realize my jaw has dropped open, and I snap it shut. John looks amazing. One hundred percent my kind of man. He's clean-shaven, his hair is neatly trimmed, and he smells faintly like woodsmoke.

I search for something to say. "Why's there snow on your boots?"

"Went out back before I knocked. Checked that dining room window and the window over the sink. Made sure they were locked tight."

"You were checking up on me?"

"Yup." John grins again. "You gonna get a jacket? Or are you not hungry yet?"

There's no way I can eat with these butterflies beating around in my belly, but I don't think I can handle sitting with him in the house, thinking about last night in the bathroom, blushing red as a tomato.

"One second." I grab my coat, purse, and keys. John waits on the porch.

I lock up, and then I look up at him. His lips are still curved.

"You got the ring?"

"Yup."

"No one got hurt, did they?"

"It turned out all right." John walks me to his truck, opens the door, and hands me up to the running board. "I'll give you the ring after."

"Are you holding it for collateral? I'll go to dinner with you. I said I would." I settle in, click the buckle. The cab smells like him. Plus a hint of gasoline.

"You're in my ride now. You're goin' where I take you."

It's silly, but my lower belly tightens, and a throb starts between my legs. "To Broyce's Bar and Grille?"

"Wherever I want, woman." He mugs a mean face. "Yeah. Broyce's. Unless you changed your mind. We could always drive up to Pyle."

I roll my eyes. "I don't want to spend an hour in the car to get three shrimp and two pieces of cucumber artfully arranged on a scoop of rice."

"Phew." John playfully wipes his brow. "I'm relieved your tastes haven't changed."

Oh, they haven't. My insides are swishing and swirling like crazy. He's so close, and he's so big. And I always loved watching him drive. The casual way he rests his hand on the steering wheel. The way he shifts. The way he glances at me out of the side of his eyes.

There's something about the way a man drives a big truck. The way *this* man drives a truck. Even when we first met he was like this. Capable, confident. And now that he's also ripped? It's heady stuff.

I feel delicate beside him. And squirmy.

There's a few more cars than I expect when we pull into Broyce's. It's a popular place, though. I guess it's as hopping on the weekends as it is during happy hours. The girls and I come sometimes after a hard shift for wings and poppers.

John helps me from the truck, grabbing me by the hips and hoisting me over a puddle of muddy slush before he sets me down. Lifting my weight looks like no effort to him at all. His large hands are light on my waist.

"So, are you just working out a lot, or do you do those competitions?"

"Competitions?"

"The ones where the guys get oiled up and pose in speedos?"

John snorts. "I work construction. And I do some security work at the businesses when they need me. Don't got time for posing in bikini bottoms." He shoots me a sly look. "You want me to, though, I can make that happen."

I wrinkle my nose. "Pass."

"You sure? I'd make it look good."

"I bet you would, sugar." Somehow, we've arrived at the hostess station, and a woman with Dolly Parton hair and a bedroom voice is grinning at us. She's older, but she's what my mother would call *well-kept*. "You're a prime specimen, aren't you?" She winks at me. "You better keep a tight hold on this one."

I'm suddenly aware of my hand clutching John's arm. I didn't know I'd let it venture there as we negotiated the icy parking lot. It must look strange. Him with me. Me grabbing at him.

I drop my hand, shove it in my pocket.

"What can I do for you, sugar?" The hostess beams at John. Preens.

The polite smile I wear by default turns brittle. She's only being friendly; it's her job. I don't need to feel any sort of way about good customer service. Sheesh.

John's smile is nothing but polite. "I had a reservation for seven, but we're early. Can we get a table for two?"

"Sure can. Name on the reservation?"

"Wall."

She rakes her gaze up John's body, eyes popped wide. "You sure are!" She scratches something off a seating chart and says, "Follow me. Is this a special occasion?"

Before I can answer, John says, "It will be."

The hostess trills, a genuine, silly laugh. "A night to remember, eh? You'll have to order the champagne. Fair warning. It's been in the back since the millennium. Best case scenario, it's aged nicely. Worst case, it's so bad nobody wants it."

My shoulders loosen. She really is just being sociable. Plenty of people remarked on John's size when we used to be together. I didn't mind then. It made me proud to be with him. I'm not accustomed anymore. That's all.

She seats us at a small table. John helps me take my coat off, and hangs it over the back of his chair. He always did that. My mother-in-law made my father-in-law do it so she has "more room to maneuver," so John thinks it's the way it's done. I told him it wasn't, but he didn't believe me.

I prefer a booth, but this table is all right. We're not smack dab in the middle of the room. We're actually next to the high-top tables by the bar. It's nice here, and we can see the TVs. That'll help if we don't have anything to talk about.

We used to be able to chat for hours, but we don't have those things in common anymore. The house, his family, our plans.

Last night, well, that wasn't exactly *conversation*. The butterflies in my stomach take a turn toward nauseating. I search for something to say.

Something light.

Something that won't bring up the past.

Oh, I got nothing.

At least John has his nose stuck in the menu, so he doesn't notice my loss for words. I follow his cue and scan the entrees. I can't read a word. It's too loud.

There are a lot of people here, and they're pretty raucous for so early in the evening. A nearby table has a family with three generations, all chatting away except the kids on their phones.

There's a table of women who look to be on a girls' night right next to us. One of them is recounting a story at top volume. Something about a friend named Becca who's gone too far, and thinks her "shit don't stink," and needs to be brought down a notch. The woman speaking is so animated, I can't focus on the entrees.

John shuts his menu firmly. "I'm gonna get a porterhouse. You want the filet?"

I breathe a sigh of relief. "Sure."

"Baked potato, no sour cream?"

He remembers. My chest warms. "Yes, please."

Our waiter comes over, and John does the ordering. It's a touch heavy-handed, but it's another thing he picked up from his dad. John Sr. has very firm ideas about how a man should treat a woman. Most of his ways are more chivalrous than anything else, so I've always rolled with it.

Whoa. Did that have something to do with why John cheated?

'Cause I was his wife, the good girl he married, not a woman he could bend over some boxes in a storage room at a motorcycle club?

"What's that?" John's frowning.

"What's what?"

"That look on your face."

"Nothing."

He raises his eyebrows expectantly.

"It's nothing." I flip through the cocktails and desserts menu left on the table. I vaguely register that the women at the high-top fall quiet. It's a whispery, giggly, expectant hush.

"Hey! Hey!" The woman who'd been boozily holding forth on "that bitch" Becca is now addressing John. "The porterhouse is a bold choice."

For a moment, John doesn't seem to register that she's talking to him.

"That's a big piece of meat. Let me know if you need help with it."

Finally, he glances over at her. She makes a show of re-crossing her legs. She's wearing one of those slinky jump-suits. It's burgundy and classy and miraculously unwrinkled in the lap.

"Hayley," one of the other women admonishes her in a stage whisper. "He's *with* someone."

"I'm just being friendly." She flashes me an unnaturally white smile. "You don't mind, do you?"

I recognize her type. She's doing well for herself. She thinks she's too good for this hick town, but she hasn't caught a ride out of it yet. She's naturally blonde and skinny and confident, so when you see her, you think "pretty."

I went to school with a girl like her. Everyone did. She made my life miserable in middle school until I got lucky, and she decided I didn't exist in ninth grade.

Girls like her end up with guys who look like John does now.

Girls like her know guys like John are taken, and they try anyway.

Hayley. Stephanie.

I turn back and direct my glare at John, cranking myself up to be hurt and bitter. And he's looking back at me.

He's never stopped looking at me.

"Babe?" He reaches out his hand across the plastic table-cloth. "You want me to ask for another table? More quiet."

My gaze flashes to Hayley. She shrugs and turns back to her table.

And my brain starts buzzing, thoughts whirling around.

John waits, patient.

"Why did you ask me out?"

He lifts a shoulder. "Tryin' to get back with you." My stomach drops, but why am I surprised?

"You want to get back together?" I'm playing for time so my brain can wrap itself around...all of this.

"Yes, Mona—" The waiter swings by with our drinks, and so we fall silent, awkwardly, while he sets down a beer for John and a glass of wine for me.

As soon as he sails off, John continues, "I want back in my house. I want back in my bed. I want back in my wife." He leans forward, his brown eyes darkening.

I know this look. He wants me. And I'm working myself up about some drunk lady, and sex positions, letting jealousy and pettiness get to me.

That's all noise.

It comes down to whether I believe this.

Do I believe *him*?

Because if I do, if he wants me now, and he never stopped wanting me...Then what went wrong between us wasn't because of another woman, prettier than me, happier than me. It wasn't only because John was weak in the moment. It wasn't because he wanted out.

The realization is huge and terrible, that he set us on fire, and I fed the flame.

But there's also a small lightness swelling in my heart. And the urge to keep talking. To test this honesty.

"Were you bored with sex with me?"

He blinks, but he keeps up. "No. But I missed it."

"Did you wish I was more adventurous?"

"Yeah."

Ouch. I breathe through it. Take a long sip of Pinot.

"I don't know. Maybe 'adventurous' ain't the word. We was tryin' to make a baby. It was different, you know? I mean, we fucked a lot, and you was always in the mood, and that was great, don't get me wrong. But I missed how it was before."

"How was it before?"

He flashes me a lazy smile. "Fuckin' awesome."

I shift in my seat. A gush of wet heat tickles between my legs. I cross my arms to hide my nipples. I should have worn a cami under this sweater. "Yeah?"

"You know. You was there."

"What made it awesome?"

John raises his beer to his lips. His eyes are twinkling. I swear—his chest is puffed out. "You did."

I roll my eyes.

"I'm a big man." He pauses, sets his beer down gently on

the table. "But I never felt as big as when you were naked under me, lookin' up with those beautiful brown eyes, legs spread, bitin' your lower lip to stop the squeal when I tried to get into your tight pussy. Damn, you were always slick as hell, but it was still a trick to get inside."

My mouth's wide open, catching flies.

"You'd wriggle that ass, buck those hips, grab the base of my cock and try to jam me in your pussy. So damn hungry for me. You were always in your head—still are, seems to be—but not when we were fucking. You just wanted what I had to give you." He's grinning, and his eyes are kind of dreamy and far away.

"And then you'd cum. Squeeze my cock like a vise. And then you'd immediately go limp and then curl up like a shrimp. Go totally dopey. Babble nonsense at me like you was makin' sense." His grin widens. "It's kind of a heady feelin', fucking a woman speechless."

I click my cheek. "I made perfect sense. You weren't hearing right. Because of my—" I can't say *any* of those words he uses. "My—"

"Hungry pussy?"

"Lustiness!"

He cracks up. "You a wench at the Renaissance festival?" John's brother Jesse jousts, so we've been more than once watching him compete. Perform? Ride his horse in dress up. It's not quite our scene, but we always have fun.

Huh. When did I get to "have fun" instead of "had fun?"

"What's goin' on in that brain of yours now?"

"You never used to ask me what I'm thinking all the time."

"That was a mistake. I don't intend to repeat it."

Thankfully, our meals arrive, and I get a few seconds to chew on that and all the rest. I'm flushed head to toe, and

I'm swollen and achy between the legs. Good thing I wore relatively thick jeans. My brain's a jumble.

Sex was different after we lost Peanut. Trying to get pregnant that first time was nothing but fun. Like John would be sitting on the sofa, watching football, and he'd unzip his pants and say, "Come make a baby with me." I'd laugh, scamper over, and I'd ride him while he nibbled my neck and kept his eyes on the score. We'd do it again that night. And the next morning.

After Peanut, I downloaded an app that tracked my cycle. I bought a fancy basal thermometer, and after sex, instead of going stupid, I'd roll to my back and tuck up my knees. And after Jellybean...I don't really remember the sex that well.

"There. That frown. What's that?" John's mumbling around a mouthful of steak.

I shake myself and grab my silverware.

"Well?"

I don't want to ruin things by bringing up the babies. But I don't want to lie. I start cutting my filet. Even though I'm not hungry, it smells delicious, and the knife slides through like butter.

"You can tell me you don't want to say. But don't block me out." John locks his eyes on mine, fork in one hand, beer in the other.

"I don't want to bring us down."

"You can't bring me down. I'm eatin' steak with my woman, and I'm gonna get lucky later. And if I ain't mistaken, there's a chocolate cake with my name on it that I didn't get a chance at last night."

"You think you're getting lucky later?"

"I'm lucky now."

"I was thinking about how things changed after Peanut."
Wow. It's the first time I've said the nickname in four years.

John carefully sets his fork down. For a minute, I think
he's going to reach for my hand, but he doesn't. He leans
back slightly in his chair, and he waits. Listening.

"Sex wasn't much fun after." John winces. Uncomfortable heat floods my face. "I'm not putting that on you. You
didn't change. I—"

I don't know how to put it into words. I felt an urgency
the second time we tried that wasn't there before. Like I was
a general, and I had to marshal all my troops and equipment
'cause this time, things were *serious*.

"I panicked. And I don't think I ever stopped panicking."
Not until John was gone. And it still flares up. Ghost panic.

I'm staring at the napkin in my lap. I can't look at the
man across the table—who's John, but who's not John
anymore now that he's chiseled and super-fit and ogled by
everyone in the place. Not when I'm unsteady from
remembering.

I take a bite of steak and chew.

Silence stretches between us.

Utensils ping against our plates.

"I didn't know what to do. I went along with the tracking
and all 'cause I thought it'd make you feel better, but it
didn't, and I didn't say shit 'cause it's not like I could fix it.
There was nothin' I could do to make you feel good again."

"Is that why you did it? Why you cheated? Because you
were mad at me because I wouldn't cheer up?" My voice
wobbles. I can't believe the waterworks aren't flowing by
now, but there's a strange peace around us. Like the eye of a
storm.

"God, no." John shifts in his seat. "I mean, yeah, I was
angry. All the time. But not at you."

"Maybe you were angry at me but you couldn't admit it. Like, it's messed up to be angry at the depressed lady who lost her baby, right?"

John winces. A flash of pain crosses his face, and he braces himself in his chair. "I was *not* angry at you. I was angry. I was angry that we kept losing the babies, that there was nothing I could do, that I was workin' this job where everyone keeps calling you a hero, but you can't stop dreaming about the time you were too late."

He must be tightening his fists in his lap because all his muscles tense in sharp relief. I want to reach for him, but I'm scared.

"I was angry twenty-four seven. Nothin' was right, and there was nothin' I could do. And, baby, I know it's no excuse, but I started drinking whiskey at five when we got back to the clubhouse. I ain't even been that drunk before. I got in a fight with Dan. Remember Dan?"

I nod. Dan was a jerk. He told me to smile literally every time I saw him.

"Baby, I was so drunk, I *lost* a fight to Dan Neuhouser."

That's impossible. Even back then, John would have outweighed him by fifty pounds.

"He landed an uppercut, I lost my balance, fell over, and decided to stay down."

John was never much of a drinker. A few beers at a picnic, that was basically it. I vaguely remember that he started drinking Wild Turkey at night after we lost Lemon, but it was a hazy time.

"Eventually, I hauled my ass up. Stephanie came looking for me." He stops. "Do you really wanna hear this?"

My grip on my fork tightens so much the metal bites into my finger. "Yes."

"She, uh, fussed over me. Put her hand on my dick.

Made herself clear." He exhales a long sigh. "And I remember thinking: what does it matter? It's all come to shit. And I did it, and the instant it was over, I puked in a corner. And I looked back, and I realized I just destroyed my life." He snaps. "Like that."

John stares over my shoulder into the middle distance, his jaw clenched, his body stiff. His regret is clear to read on his face.

And part of me is angry. Belligerent. *He* made it all come to shit. He destroyed *my* life.

And another part of me, the pieces that could never stop loving John Wall, wants to go back in time and say I'll come with you on the ride. I won't let you get drunk and fight some idiot. I won't let you be alone in your grief like I chose to be alone in mine.

He's right. There's no excuse. But I don't know if you need a good excuse to forgive someone. Maybe forgiving is something you do. And then the rest follows.

"Baby." John breaks the silence. "I'm so sorry I didn't know what to do."

I drag in a shaky breath. "I didn't know what to do, either."

We fall quiet, but this silence is different. Mellowed. After John finishes his steak, he slides his asparagus onto my plate. I polish it off. It's soaked in butter, the perfect balance of crisp and cooked.

At some point, I realize the table of women has left. I didn't even notice them go.

The waiter comes back to ask if we want dessert. I'm at a loss. I don't want this to end, this raw but amiable peace. However, my body's strung tight. I don't think I can bear to sit much longer.

"Ain't there chocolate cake at home?" John puts the ball in my court.

It's my decision.

A part of me wants to call it a night, retreat, regroup, and patch my defenses back together. But it's Saturday night. It's only six thirty. Sure, I have wine and hard seltzers and study guides at home. And laundry. I have things I could do.

None of it sounds nearly as good as chocolate cake.

I don't mind being alone, but I want to be with John Wall.

"Okay," I say. "Let's go home."

John's smile engulfs his whole face. "Check, please."

As soon as John pays, he morphs into a different man. He was a gentleman before, patient, calm, cool, and collected. Now? He's a man on a mission.

He puts me in my coat, zips it up to my nose, grips my hand tightly in his, and rushes me out the door.

"John?" I'm trying to go slow. The dropping temps have frozen the slush puddles.

He half-mutters, half-growls, wraps his arm around my waist, and hoists me to his hip. In a few giant strides, we're at the truck.

I'm breathless, the frigid air burning my lungs. But I feel light, too. Giddy.

John nearly flings me into the cab, pausing a second to skewer me with burning eyes which send a sizzle down my spine. "Buckle up."

In seconds, he's behind the wheel, and we're pulling off onto the highway. It's freezing—he didn't wait to warm up the engine at all—and it's so funny. He's drumming on the steering wheel, flipping the radio from station to station, checking on me every half-second, but he is not letting the odometer go a mile past the speed limit.

We get passed by a guy in a Buick Skylark from the 90s.

"What are you grinning at?" John narrows his twinkling eyes. "That man's a maniac."

"He was going at least fifty-six."

"Right? Madman."

My lips twitch, and my jangly nerves begin to settle. The next time John fiddles with the radio, I swat his hand away. "Leave it."

We listen to old-timey country the rest of the ride, and by the time we pull up to the house, the urgency's gone, and we've gotten shy again.

John's slow to come for me, his boots crunching in the snow. It's dark now, and the moon is shining.

I take his hand. We walk together to the front door. He stops us on the porch. He cups my jaw with a calloused palm.

"You gonna let me in, baby?" His hand slips down to wrap around the back of my neck. He tilts my head back and drops a soft kiss on the corner of my mouth.

"Yes," I exhale. It has the power of a starter pistol.

Somehow, he has the key, and he's throwing open the door, edging me inside, and then my back's to the wall, and his shirt's unbuttoned, and my sweater's on the floor and my hair is standing on end from the static electricity.

I try to smooth it down, and he steps back, taking me in. My breasts are heaving from trying to catch my breath. We're in the middle of the dimly-lit living room, the only light coming from the corner lamp I always leave on.

He's wearing a sleeveless undershirt. Oh, wow. Veins run down his bulging biceps and his solid forearms. His shoulders and his pecs are cut; even his neck is corded with muscle. His body is amazing.

I choke out a gulp. He grins.

He sees where I'm staring, and he flexes his pecs, making them twitch like they've been zapped. I giggle; I can't help it.

He grins wider and does it again. Happy I'm happy. Like a silly kid.

Then his fingers drop to the button of his pants. My mouth waters. My breath catches. And then his hand falls to his side. Oh. He's changed his mind. No. I follow his gaze. He hasn't thought better of this; he's completely enthralled by my breasts.

My nipples were already hard, but they tighten and chafe against the lace of my bra. He groans. My fingers fly up to the swells that spill out of the cups.

"Yes," he exhales, closing the space between us in one, long stride, taking my face in his hands, gently easing my neck back so I meet his eyes.

"You want this, Mona?"

Oh. What? Yes? My mind's a fuzzy swirl, and chills are racing down my bare belly while heat pulses in my core.

John lowers his mouth and tugs at my lower lip, but he doesn't linger. He peppers my jaw with kisses, and then he brushes more across my nose. I giggle. Just a little. He knows I'm ticklish.

"Can I take this off?" His hands have migrated behind my back, and he's unclasping my bra.

I don't have the breath anymore to answer, so I nod.

He undoes each hook, and then eases it down my arms. His breath is coming fast now, too, his magnificent chest rising and falling. His face is greedy with anticipation.

I arch my back, stretching my spine, raising my breasts,

offering them to him. I want to drive him wild. Like I used to.

He moans.

"Baby, you're so fucking beautiful."

His hands settle at my hips, and he grips me tight, his eyes darting feverishly between my aching breasts and my lips.

"I want to kiss you for real, baby. Can I kiss you? You got to know, if I start, I don't want to stop. Okay, baby?"

Oh....Yes. I think? Unsettling zings of fear compete with the heat and the longing. In the last few hours, my emotions have been pinging back and forth like a pinball, and I don't quite know if they've stopped.

John's overwhelming, and he's not going anywhere.

His grip tightens. You know what? I don't have to fight. I don't have to be mad and uncertain anymore. I can open up. Give in.

"I want inside, baby. Let me inside."

My nipples pucker, and my pussy spasms.

"Okay," I whisper.

And he smiles, the biggest I've seen since I came to him at the clubhouse, and he doesn't waste a second, cradling the nape of my neck and wrapping his other arm around my butt, scooting me fully into his embrace, taking my mouth, gently, insistently, teasing my lips apart and sliding his tongue past my teeth to taste me, test me, tease me until I remember the rhythm, too.

And then I'm kissing John Wall. And he's even hungrier, even more demanding than he used to be. It's the same, but it feels like the stakes are infinitely higher.

He lifts me effortlessly, and he carries me to the bedroom, not once stopping the kiss, and I'm floating, my heart, my hopes, everything.

He still tastes like fresh, morning air. I don't know why, but he always has.

We get to the bed and he lays me on my back, straddles me with those enormous thighs, and then he bends to take a nipple in his mouth, suckling, tugging, as he struggles with his pants.

Each drag of his mouth sends tingles to my pussy. He knows how sensitive my breasts are. He lavishes one, and then he suckles the other, sweeping and swirling his tongue, rasping the nipple until I can't stand it, my hips bucking of their own accord while his big, rough hands cup, mold, and knead.

His chest is there, and I rake my fingers down it, test the hardness, the strength through the cotton. He groans, dropping kisses on my belly, working his way down my body.

I gasp. I know where he's heading. "John. I don't—Uh, I didn't—"

I was never one hundred percent cool with oral sex. It felt good, the way he did it, but I always worried so much about how I smelled and if he was grossed out—although John always said he loved tasting me. But I'd never let things go that direction unless I was fresh out of the shower. Most times, I shut him down.

"It's okay, baby. Let me make you feel good."

"But I'm—"

"Perfect. So sexy."

He tugs off my boots, and peels down my panties with my jeans, and then he inhales deeply, his face burrowing in my curls. He's careful not to touch my injured knee, still bandaged but feeling better. He lifts my other leg, placing it over his enormous, rock hard shoulder.

"But John," I pant, my nails digging into his rock-hard shoulders.

The flat of his tongue swoops from the bottom to the top of my slit, raspy and hot, eager, relentless. He's lapping, and his blunt fingers are everywhere, holding me open, popping my clit from its hood. He sucks hard, swirls his tongue, but he has no rhythm, and he doesn't linger. He's eating me, feasting, pleasing himself, grunting.

His prickly cheeks chafe my thighs, and he nips at my swollen pussy lips. He's like an animal.

Okay, he definitely doesn't have a problem with how I smell. And no matter how I taste, I think he loves it. Tension I wasn't aware I was holding leaves my body. He must feel my legs turn to jelly because he cocks his head and grins at me from between my legs.

"Want me to stop?"

"No." Without a second thought, I push his head back down, and he laughs.

"Okay, baby."

He dives back in, his stiff tongue plunging into my core and then lapping and rasping over my lips, inside my folds, his thumb circling my clit whenever his tongue ventures south. His other hand is wandering, teasing my nipples, gripping my waist.

My hips are rising, chasing that tongue, and I realize I'm grinding against his face. I try to stop, but he snarls, and he brings his wandering hand between my legs, slip sliding his fingers through my slickness, and then he begins circling my bottom hole.

I gasp. My legs reflexively clench, but I can't close them. He's a solid brace.

I used to like this sometimes. When I'd had a few glasses of wine. But I'm totally sober now.

And it still feels good.

He applies more pressure with his ring finger, as he

eases his thick index finger into my pussy, laving my clit with the rough flat of his tongue. My channel contracts. The finger at my bottom is insistent, pressing past the tight ring of muscle, easing in, making me feel full and vulnerable and dirty. But in the best way.

"Good girl," he mutters in my ear. "Let me in."

He slips another finger into my pussy, pumping, and wet noises fill the air. I'm hot with embarrassment, but he's so heavy, I can't dislodge him, and somehow that makes the shyness go away. There's no help for it. He's so big; he can do what he wants to me.

My belly tightens, my clit aches, and the finger in my bottom is insistent. I have no choice but to let him in, and my mind lets go.

I want more.

Two fingers aren't enough. I take my hands from where I'd mindlessly dug them into his hair to urge him on, and I grab the shoulder of his undershirt, tugging upwards.

He rises immediately, the most crestfallen look on his face. Instantly, it's replaced with a cocky grin as I shove down his jeans and his boxers, freeing his hard, red cock, veiny and thick. That's what I want.

I whimper.

"You sure, baby?" He's braced above me on his arms, gliding his huge, hot cock over the swollen spot sensitized by his sucking and tonguing and stubble.

I guide him to where I want him, and he doesn't need any more encouragement. He drives home, stretching me—it's been a really long time—and then drawing back to pound home again, hard, like I want, keeping time with the crazy bucking of my hips.

"Cum on my cock, Mona," he orders, slamming to the base, his forehead looming over mine, eyes screwed shut, sweat beading his brow. He's braced on his forearms, as if it's no effort, all that glorious muscle flexing. All I can do is hold on for the ride.

He's hitting the spot. All the spots. He's so thick, and he remembers how I like it. No holds barred. He turns me into a rag doll, driving me up the bed until I hit the headboard. I make a little oof, and he moves his forearm to protect my head, all the while stoking the fire that swirls and swirls until it explodes, and as my muscles spasm on his cock, he roars, filling me with his hot cum.

Oh, crap.

I'm not on the pill!

Panic flutters to life in my chest as my limbs goes limp. John stares down at me, worry hooding his eyes.

"Don't panic," he says.

He's not moving. He came in me. I should go...uh... taking a shower doesn't help. I know that. Morning after pill. Freezing dread creeps up my spine.

"You're panicking."

"I'm not on the pill."

"We'll go to the pharmacy in the morning. You can breathe, Mona."

"I can't. You weigh five hundred pounds."

"You're hurtin' my feelings, woman." He still rolls over, but he pulls me with him, cuddling me to his chest. "How about we freak out about this tomorrow?"

"Are you freaking out?" I squirm, but his enormous hands hold me in place.

"Nope."

"You're not?" He nudges my head until my ear is pressing against his chest. His undershirt is damp with sweat. His heart's definitely beating fast, but not crazy fast. And it slows as I listen.

"Why aren't you freaking out?" I whisper.

"Too tired." He grunts, and then the big lug has the audacity to fall asleep. Never mind the mess. Our mistake. He's out cold in sixty seconds.

It takes me a little longer, but not much. I drift off to the sound of his heart, steady and sure, as his warmth surrounds me.

I WAKE UP, groggy and disoriented, hours later. Someone's rummaging in the linen closet. The hallway light is on.

John?

It comes rushing back. I'm naked and sticky, tucked neatly under the covers. I listen a few more seconds. Those are John's footsteps. He must be looking for a blanket. Instead of heading back to bed, though, he pads toward to door to the garage.

Is this a nail and bail? I fight to sit up as my stomach sinks. But John parked on the street. He's leaving through the wrong door if he's making his escape. I only use the garage for storage.

Besides, now that I'm looking around, his shirt, under-shirt, and boots are on the floor. What's he doing?

I slide my feet into a pair of fuzzy slippers and tie on a robe. Whatever he's up to, it's not clandestine. He's making no effort to be stealthy.

He left the door to the garage open, and the bare light-bulb overhead is on. He's back by the metal shelving where I keep the Christmas ornaments.

"John?"

I cross to him, and his face emerges from the shadows.

His hair's sticking up, and there's a bleak expression on his face. He has a teal plastic tub in his hands.

"I'm sorry I woke you." His voice is gritty with sleep. His eyes are red. Maybe it's not from sleep.

"What are you looking for?" I step closer, and rest my hand on the tub.

He clears his throat. "The blanket my ma knitted. I wasn't gonna take it or nothin'. I just wanted to see it. If you kept it."

Of course I kept it. I take the tub from him. He lets me. I set it on the picnic table I brought in for the winter.

I haven't looked in the tub since I packed it up, but I know exactly what's in it. A stuffed rabbit John and I bought at a little boutique in Pyle when we went to dinner to celebrate finding out about Peanut. A congratulations card from his parents. We waited to tell mine—good thing—but we had to tell Ma and Pa Wall. A half-dozen little outfits because Ma Wall couldn't help herself. A sonogram. A sympathy card.

Another sonogram. No cards. We didn't tell anyone with Jellybean.

And then two more sonograms. No card. We were all so much more superstitious with Lemon. But then we passed the twelve-week mark, and Ma Wall presented us with a beautiful, crocheted blanket, a pastel rainbow with an adorable yellow bunny rabbit on it.

The blanket's on the top. I hand it to John.

"You can have it, if you want." It kills me to say it.

"No, baby. I just wanted to see it. I knew you had it somewhere."

It was hard to put the things in the garage. I'd had them in my bedroom closet, but seeing the tub every day when I got my clothes was too hard.

John unfolds the blanket and holds it up. His wingspan is so wide he can hold it taut.

"Ma made each of us one exactly like it. But a different animal. Mine's lost. I had a green rabbit. Kellum had a chick. Can't remember what Cashel and Jesse had, but one of 'em had a turtle. Dina had a duck."

He sniffs the blanket for a second, folds it neatly, and returns it to the tub. It's then I notice the ink on his chest. He has lots of tattoos—the skull and hammer, the flaming bike, the ax and hatchet and American flag—but this is new. Right over his heart. A design that's mostly rose and partly thorns, and hidden in the swirls, a peanut, a blue jellybean, and a lemon.

I close the space between us and trace the outline of the rose. John stands completely still.

He wanted a family so badly. So did I. He always talked about how he wanted to see a bunch of kids nipping at my heels like baby ducklings.

Oh, lord. He was hurting so bad back then. I *knew*. But it felt like another failure. I shoved it away. I shoved him away. I couldn't save him when I was drowning.

"I'm sorry," I mumble into his broad, bare chest. I pray he doesn't ask me what for. Too many things.

He raises my hand and brushes my knuckles with a kiss. "You know what would help me get back to sleep?"

"What?"

"Chocolate cake."

It's a lifeline, and I'll take it. I let him shelve the tub and lead me to the kitchen. I pour him a big glass of milk and cut him a thick piece of cake.

We don't go back to sleep. We whisper about all sorts of nonsense until the sun comes up, snuggled on the sofa, as if nothing changed, when everything is different.

# 8

## WALL

It's almost six o'clock in the evening when I pull into the cul-de-sac to Mona's house. *Our* house.

I took the long way home. Instead of Route 12, I rode along the river, crossing at the old truss bridge on Saltpeter Road. It's bitter cold, and despite the gloves, my hands are frozen solid.

I needed the ride to get my head straight. I told Mona I'd be back after work, but I don't know what I'm walkin' into, and truth be told, I'm raw.

It ain't like Mona and I talked everything out. Last night, she told me all about nursing and her plans, and I told her about working construction, and then for some reason I told her about the coyote, and that started us both off on stories about animals, which led us to dogs we'd known, and then we'd drifted off.

She could meet me at the door and tell me it was a mistake.

She could not open the door at all.

I had nerves of steel yesterday at dinner. Now? When I got everything at stake? Not so much.

I back my bike into the driveway, grateful it's not calling for more snow. I don't like to leave my bike out in this weather, but it'll be fine for a few hours.

Hopefully, I'll get a few hours. I don't know what I'm gonna do if she asks me to take her to the pharmacy. Or if I see she's already been.

I take off my helmet, crack my neck, and stretch my back. I'm draggin' my feet.

The front door opens. My breath catches in my chest.

Mona pushes open the storm door, but she doesn't step out. She's showered. She took the time to dry her hair in those waves she likes, and she's wearing a flannel shirt and yoga pants that hug her curves just so. My mouth waters.

She stares at me, her mouth turned down at the corners.

I stay where I am.

"You came back." She worries at her bottom lip.

"Yeah. I said I would." I suddenly remember the ring and dig it out of my pocket. I never did give it to her last night. "Got it." I hold it up. Her face falls.

"Oh. Um. Thanks. I, uh. Let me get my shoes on. I'll come get it."

My chest tightens. No. That door's half open. She's done her hair. That's not how this is goin' down.

I stride forward with purpose, and she puts on her brave face. Fuck that.

I said if I ever got a chance with her again, I'd speak my piece. I wouldn't keep on, keepin' on, and let everything fall apart around me.

"Mona, I want to come in the house."

She firms that cute, pointy chin. "Did you leave something?"

"Yeah, I left something." If she's gonna be dense, I'm gonna be blunt.

I take a step, and like most people, she gives way. So I take another. We're in the foyer now. "I left a pretty girl with the sweetest smile who was happy to be curled up next to me. Where'd she go?"

I squint into the corners, playing around. Her mouth twitches at the corner before the shadows reappear in her eyes. "You got the ring. Thank you. We're...even. You don't have to hang around."

My gut sours. "This ain't about being even."

"It's not?" Her voice is breathy. Hopeful. Scared.

"Let me back in, Mona."

She shoots a glance behind me at the door. "You're already in."

"*All* the way in. I promise, I ain't gonna fuck things up again." I hold up the ring.

The look on her face is the scariest shit I've ever seen. Pain. Fear. Grief. Resignation. And then she really looks at the ring.

"It's pretty."

"Yeah."

And then she really looks at me.

"I'm scared."

I almost say don't be. I almost say I won't let anything bad happen. Instead, I say, "Me, too."

She takes the ring. "I'll put this in my purse. Miss Janice is going to be so happy."

I follow her into the kitchen, and as soon as she's zippered it into her wallet, I swing her into my arms and head for the stairs.

"What are you doing?" She lets herself smile. She knows what I'm doin'.

"I'm fixin' to make you happy."

She giggles and halfheartedly tries to wriggle loose.

She's a good, solid armful, but she's got no chance against me.

"Put me down."

"I will." I haul her to the bedroom, dumping her on the bed. She bounces. Those beautiful tits bounce, and those soft wavy curls. She's full blown smilin' now. There's a little eagerness beginning to glow in her eyes.

That's my girl.

You know, thinkin' about it, there weren't any tire tracks in the snow, and there was still a dusting of snow on the roof of her car. She didn't go to the pharmacy while I was gone.

My chest floods with warmth as I take her mouth and settle between her legs. She softens under me, lets me in. I taste her, tangle with her tongue, breathe in her scent. I can't describe how good it is. It's Mona.

All I ever wanted.

First time I met Mona, I was at a bonfire with some guys from my fire academy class. They were looking for easy pussy, and I wouldn't have turned it down. The girls were skewing a little young for me, though.

And then I saw Mona. She was smiling, shy and quiet, perched on a log, hiding herself beside her loud ass girl-friend. She was wearing a puffy vest and boots, dressed the exact same as every other girl there, but to me, she stood out as bright as the fire.

She seemed a little lost, a little overwhelmed, a little excited. Her face hid nothing. I couldn't do anything but stare and stand nearby like a dumbass, nursing my beer, trying to find an opening, but her friend was too damn chatty.

Finally, Mona finished her beer and whispered some-thing to her friend. The friend waved her off into the bushes. She had to piss. Mona wrinkled that adorable nose.

Guess she didn't like the idea of popping a squat in the woods. She sat there awhile longer, and then she whispered to the friend again, but the friend had scored herself a man, and she wasn't budging.

Finally, Mona ventured off into the shadows. More than a few pairs of eyes followed her. A guy from my program, a real dog, made a move in her direction.

I beat him to it. I remember exactly how it went down.

*I call out to her from a yard or so behind, "I don't want you to think I'm a pervert or nothin', but I'm gonna be here behind you at a respectful distance. I'm John Wall. My mama would whoop me if I let a woman wander around alone in the dark."*

*There's silence and rustling. I can't see her. It's a cloudy night.*

*"I'm Mona." Her voice, soft and nervous, goes straight to my dick. "It's really dark out here."*

*"Yup. Be careful where you step."*

*"I have to pee real bad." She's slurring her words.*

*"I figured."*

*"I've never peed outside before."*

*"Can't say the same. It easier for a man, though."*

*"I'm really drunk."*

*"Yeah. Be careful. Maybe try to find an incline."*

*"An incline?" She giggles from somewhere off in the brush.*

*"Yeah, you know. Face uphill."*

*"Are you giving me pointers on squatting to pee?" That giggle again. So sweet. "From your vast experience?"*

*"Whenever I squat to piss in the woods, I find an incline. You do with that information what you will. Far be it for me to tell a woman what to do."*

*She laughs, and then she comes crashing toward me, buttoning her jeans. She wasn't lyin' about being drunk. She was hiding it well, sitting on the log back by the fire, but she's three sheets to the wind.*

*She careens into me, and I steady her with my arms. She feels amazing, warm and curvy. She rises up on her toes. "I guess I'm being ungrateful. Thank you for the advice, John Wall."*

*She's staring at my lips.*

*I'm basking in it all. She smells like woodsmoke and vanilla, and her tits are brushing my chest, her smile beaming at me in the dark.*

*I want to kiss her. I want to take her home, unwrap her like a present, and keep her smiling and giggling in my arms. But tonight, she's drunk, and I ain't gonna take advantage.*

*A frown steals across her face. Whatever caused it, I'm gonna kick its ass.*

"Oh, crud. Do you know what time it is?"

*I check my phone.* "Eleven."

*She exhales, happy again.* "Oh, good. I have another hour. I should drink some water." *She sighs and hiccups at the same time.* "Actually, who am I kidding. My parents aren't waiting up. I'll be fine."

*Oh, shit.*

"How old are you, Mona?"

*She's got a grown woman's tits. Fuck.*

"Seventeen. Almost." *She grins and wriggles closer to me. My arms can't help but hold her tight.* "How old are you?"

"Twenty-one."

*I do the hardest thing I've ever done. I drop my arms, but as I do, I grab her hand. It's dark. She could trip and hurt herself.*

"Does this mean you're not gonna kiss me?" *Her voice is genuinely sad, not bratty in the least.*

"I'll kiss you in a year or so." *I lead her back the fire.* "Is your ride the girl you've been sitting next to?"

"Abby? Yeah."

"She's drunk. I'll drive you both home."

*She's quiet a minute. "Will you drop me home last?" she finally asks.*

*"That's what I was planning on."*

We talked in the cab of my truck 'til the sun came up. She was right. Her parents didn't notice she was hanging out with a strange man in their driveway.

I didn't want to let her go that morning.

I've never wanted to let her go.

But she left me when she was grieving the babies. She wandered off in the dark, and I couldn't find her. I was stupid and weak, and I fucked up. I almost ruined everything forever.

But here she is. Soft and squirming underneath me. Taking my cock, crying out my name. Still the most beautiful woman I've ever seen.

I can't screw this up again.

She didn't go to the pharmacy.

She's trusting me again, and she has less of a reason now than when we were at that bonfire. I need to be strong.

And I'm fucking terrified.

## 9

## MONA

Miss Janice twists the ring on her finger as I read to her from Proverbs. I keep both hands on the book, resisting the constant urge to rest my hand on my belly. I missed my period, and there's a weird taste in my mouth all the time. I'm pregnant. The test I took before I came to work confirmed it.

I haven't told John yet. And he hasn't been around long enough to know my cycle.

For the past three days, since I began to suspect, I've been terrified twenty-four seven.

The floor is quiet. It's midnight, and most of the residents are asleep. Nursing homes are never totally silent, but there's less bustle from food services and OT and visitors. Every time a door shuts or someone coughs, I startle.

Miss Janice doesn't seem to notice. Her insomnia is acting up, so I'm keeping her company for a few minutes before I leave. I'm on second shift this week. I switched with Lorraine so she can deal with some issues with her kid's school.

John's at a clubhouse party. It's fine. We talked about it.

There was a poker run today with his old club, Smoke and Steel, and a bonfire afterward with a local band.

John's going to call me after my shift, and he'll come home if things get too wild. It's fine. I'm okay with it. We talked about it at length. In the past few weeks, I've gone to the clubhouse for some daytime events, and I've gone for some rides with his brothers and their old ladies. Dizzy and Fay-Lee. Pig Iron and Deb. They're cool. Not my usual type of person, but interesting.

As I sit here and read, my gut's churning, but that's probably because I forgot my packed lunch and got a tray from food service. I trust John. He does everything he can to reassure me. There's no lock on his phone, and he's always handing it to me to look up something when we're driving somewhere. Like he doesn't know where the turn off to Lake Patonquin is.

He tells me where he's going to be, and who's going to be there. I've never heard of such a crazy cast of characters—Forty, Plum, Boots, Big George, whose real name is Clark, and a guy name Bullet who has a little girl called Squick. Poor thing.

He loves these people, though. And they seem to think the world of him. So, I like them, too.

It's strange. It's almost like I've split John into three people in my mind. There's the man I met when I was sixteen. Then, there's the man who cheated on me. I still don't understand that person at all. And then there's this guy. This guy's still playful, but he's serious, too. Even though he's built like the Hulk, he seems wary. Like he's always on defense, bracing himself.

He's not the same man I married. He's...weathered. Cautious with me. Grim, sometimes. And in bed, he's *starving*. He doesn't stop until I'm a wrung out, boneless mass, and he scoops me into his strong arms, and he strokes my back and kisses me until I fall asleep.

Sometimes, I wake up in the middle of the night, and he's still cradling me, rubbing circles at the base of my spine —which always aches after work—watching sports on mute.

I feel like we've been through the war together, and like I still don't know him at all.

And I'm totally lying to myself. My stomach is queasy as hell. I don't like that he's at a party without me at an MC clubhouse. And I hate, hate, hate that I'm worried.

And I am scared *shitless* about the pregnancy.

If I posted on one of those internet advice boards— having unprotected sex with my ex who cheated on me, and I'm pregnant—I'd be roasted. If I told anyone, they'd judge me, and they'd be right. What business do I have bringing a new life into such a messy situation?

I thought I was old enough; I'd made all my dumb mistakes already. Nope.

I kept thinking that I'd call the doctor. Or go down that aisle of the grocery store. But I didn't. And as soon as John comes home—and no matter what he's got planned for his day, he comes to me as soon as he's done—he wraps his arms around me, inhales as if I'm apple pie straight out of the oven, and then he's eating me up, and I lose my mind.

I've missed him. To the *bone*. And it kills me to wonder if I had to miss him this long.

But what if I'd tried to work through it with John? Would I have discovered the other things? When I'm only taking courses in nursing, not English and history, I'm good at school. I love elder care. I don't need someone to be behind me to make something of myself.

Although I *am* grateful for my cheerleaders. Speaking

of, Miss Janice is wide awake and starting to root around in her bag of whatnots. I think she's had enough of the good book.

I slip in a postcard to mark our place. "Save the rest for another night?"

"All right. Have you seen my cheaters?"

I reach out and pluck them from her head. "These cheaters?"

"Am I that predictable?"

"Sure are."

"Do you have to get going?"

"Nope." I'm not looking forward to sitting at home, waiting for John to come back from a party. Too much déjà vu. Maybe I should text him and suggest he crash at the clubhouse. But can my nerves take that? My stomach gurgles.

"Are you hungry? I have some peanut chews."

Oh. Gross. No. I swallow hard. "No, thanks. I'll grab a snack when I get home."

"Your man going to be waiting up?" Miss Janice's eyes twinkle.

"How did you know I had a man?"

"Nurse gossip. He dropped you off on his motorcycle the other day. Francine said she hoped you knew what to do with all that man."

I bust out laughing. Francine is Miss Janice's pinochle friend on the night shift. "You can assure Francine that I do."

"Where'd you meet him? Heck, when did you have the time?"

I glance down at my lap. I'm a private person, but I'm not comfortable telling a bold-faced lie.

"He's my husband."

Miss Janice's eyes go round. "You lose your ring, too?"

I wiggle my bare fingers. My ring is in my jewelry box. "We've been separated awhile."

"How long is awhile?"

"Four years."

"Glory day. There's a story there."

"We...ran into a rough patch. I kicked him out. He left and stayed gone. But he never sent me papers, and I didn't either."

"You were young."

"Not that young."

"*Young.*" Miss Janice sniffs. "So what did he do? Was he unfaithful?"

My face heats. I don't have to say anything.

"He's the fast type, eh?"

The idea makes me smile. "John? No. He's a homebody, really. He likes what he likes—fishing, riding, hunting, lifting. *Eating.* But I wouldn't call him fast."

"So what happened?" Miss Janice twists her ring. "You don't have to tell me if you don't want to, dear, but I've got good ears for listening. Well, the right one's good. The left one, not so much."

"You know what, Miss Janice? It's hard to say. We were going through a hard time. Both of us. We weren't talking much. Just trying to get through the day, you know? But I never thought—*never*—that he'd do that. I'd have bet anyone a million bucks he'd never cheat. And I was wrong."

The awful pain that'd gotten dull these past few weeks flashes hot and sharp in my brain. What if it never goes away? What if somehow John and I stay together, and every night he's a few minutes late, I still feel this way?

And I can hear my mother in my head. *Well, shouldn't you have thought about that before you rushed off halfcocked like you always do?*

"What does he say for himself?"

I grimace. "We talked about it once. A little. I still don't get it. I know I should talk to him."

Miss Janice laughs. "Yes. You should. I will say, though... Did I ever tell you about Lloyd and the savings account?"

"I can't say that you did."

"Well, Lloyd was in charge of the finances. I got an allowance for household expenses, and that was that. I could make a penny squeal, let me tell you."

I can't imagine, but it was a different time. My dad handles the money, too. Makes my mother ask for it every month.

"Well, when Lloyd died, come to find out, he had over half a million dollars in a savings account at Pyle National Bank."

"Holy crap. Half a million?"

"Half a million. We never talked about money, and he never told me about it."

"What did you do?"

"I was mad as hell at first. Do you know how many coupons I clipped? And store brand cream cheese is *awful*. And telling my Thomas he couldn't go do that semester overseas, or he'd have to make a pair of shoes last another year. Terrible."

"You had no idea?"

"None. I thought we were barely making it all along. I was furious for *years*."

"How did you get past it?"

"Spending some of that money helped. I went to Tuscany. Took my son and his wife, before Little Tommy was born."

"I've always wanted to go to Italy."

"It's beautiful. But I'll tell you what it took to let go of the anger. I had a few glasses of wine at a family reunion, and I got into a conversation with his sister. She got to talking, all about how they almost starved when the mill closed, and their dad lost his job. They ate grass to try to fill their bellies. Can you imagine?"

I shake my head.

"I knew times were tough when he was young, but I didn't *understand*. And we never really talked about it."

"You're not angry anymore?"

"No. But I wish I could tell him I understand. And whack him upside the head. I wish he would have trusted *us* more."

"You would have bought the store brand cream cheese for him?"

"Not even once." Miss Janice laughs, and I stand to say my goodbyes.

A wave of dizziness and nausea washes over me. I mumble my goodbyes to Miss Janice, and I barely make it to the bathroom before I throw up the remnants of my late lunch. Mostly, I'm dry heaving.

Oh, Lord. This feeling is *so* familiar. It's not normal queasiness. It's a bloated, gross barfiness that vomiting doesn't actually help. It's the worst. I flush, pee, and wipe. And I look down at the tissue—force of habit—and there's a brownish streak.

Blood.

All my blood drains to my feet. I can hear my heart pounding in the cold, empty bathroom.

Not again.

I can't breathe.

Maybe it's a mistake. I wipe again. Another streak.

I need to call John.

I wash my hands and rush off for the lockers, pulling out my phone. My fingers shake as I dial.

This can't be happening again. It has to be a mistake.

My heart thuds in my chest. I'm panicking. I need to stop. Maybe it's implantation bleeding.

I always told myself that first. Until I couldn't explain away what was happening.

I need to hear John's voice.

The phone rings.

I grab my coat and purse, waving at the nurse's station out of habit.

And rings.

Why is he not answering? Every time I call him now, he picks up on the first or second ring. That first week we were back together, I made up dumb reasons to call him. To ask him if he still liked pickled beets. Remind him that he'd left his gloves on the kitchen counter. Every time he picked right up—guys shouting in the background or trucks beeping as they back up—and my belly danced.

He's not picking up now.

Maybe he's on his bike.

But the ride ended hours ago. He texted when he got back to the clubhouse. Sent me a picture of the band.

I pause beside my car, bend over, and hack into the slushy snow. Nothing comes out, but the urge to vomit eases somewhat. My head swims.

His voicemail picks up. *This is Wall. Leave a message. Beep.*

I hit end and try to call again.

Ring.

Ring.

Ring.

*This is Wall. Leave a message. Beep.*

My palms are clammy. I shrug my jacket off. I'm sweating bullets even though it's thirty degrees out.

I need to calm down. Drive home. Then what?

I don't know "what." What have I done?

I hold myself as still as I possibly can. I had wine with dinner last Sunday. I had deli ham from food service for lunch on Monday. Before I swung by the pharmacy on Tuesday, I hadn't taken a vitamin in years. Terror and grief and guilt cascade over me. What have I done?

I call John again, more ringing. I throw the phone into the passenger seat, but it bounces onto the floor, and now I can't find it 'cause it's dark, and the inside light isn't bright enough.

I'm going to the clubhouse.

I'm going to find out why he's not answering his phone.

I turn the key and immediately a surge of energy—courage? fury?—rushes through my veins. I'm never going to pace a living room, waiting for John Wall again. I'm never calling and calling and not getting through. I'm gonna roll up to that clubhouse, and I'm gonna tell him off like I didn't the first time.

Or I'm going puke on his shoes.

Probably that.

What is John going to say if I tell him I'm pregnant, and I'm losing it again?

He asked, that day when he came back with Janice's ring. He said, "Do you want me to take you to the pharmacy?"

I said, "Did you want to go now?"

He said, "No."

And that's how we left it. Well, he scooped me off the couch, tore off my pants, and settled me on top of his dick, but we didn't talk anymore about it.

What if he's with some woman? What if that's why he's not picking up?

What if Stephanie's at the clubhouse tonight? I intentionally didn't ask if she'd be there because I trust him, right? I have to trust him, that's what you're supposed to do when you forgive someone. But what if this is history repeating itself, and I have no one to blame this time but myself?

Oh, God. History is repeating itself.

I take the turn onto Rural Route 9 too quickly, and my back wheels skid. Black ice. My heart jumps and sticks in my throat.

I need to slow down. I'm gonna throw up. There's nothing in the car to throw up into. I gag, and then I mash my lips together.

And then there's the clubhouse, the only building for miles, a blaze of lights in the pitch-black night. There are so many bikes, trucks, cars. I have to park along the road and tromp through the snow. I forgot to change from my clogs to my snow boots, so the heels of my socks get wet. I slip, cutting my knees on gravel and ice, pain shooting up my thigh.

Now I have wet pants too, sticking to my legs. I'm freezing.

My teeth chatter, and I realize I've left my coat in the car, and I'm still wearing my scrubs with the sloths that say, "No hurry. No worry."

Too late now. I'm flinging open the door, but this time, no one turns to stare. No one even notices.

There's an orgy going on.

Okay, not one big orgy, but several smaller orgies. There's a woman on the pool table buck naked, her head resting in a man's lap, her legs hanging over the sides. And a man in between them. And another man waiting in line.

I've only seen that in porn.

Has John done this? He wasn't with anyone when we got

back together, but I haven't asked him who his was with when we were split. I didn't want to know.

Did he stand in line to have sex with some stranger?

And there's a pantless man on the bar in a leather jacket and a cowboy hat, strutting back and forth, occasionally stopping to swivel his hips so his limp penis swings in circles, and there are three older gentleman—the same from the first time I came here—nursing beers, ignoring him.

The air is thick with marijuana smoke. I'm not a prude. I know it has medicinal qualities, but this is *not* a recommended dosage. I try to breathe through my mouth, as if that's somehow better.

Where is John?

Is Stephanie here?

What is my body doing?

The crowd is thick, and damn but there's dozens of young, attractive women, and every last one of them is blonde. There's a blonde who looks like a sex doll, dancing like a professional to..."That Smell?" By Lynryd Skynyrd?

There's a blonde with purple streaks rubbing up on an older man with a beer belly, blondes at the bar, blondes everywhere.

Would I even know Stephanie to look at her?

A wild rage grabs hold of me. I hope she's here. I want to punch her in the face. I want to call her a homewrecker.

God, where is John?

The smoke's burning my eyes as I push through the crowd. I don't know where I'm going. To his room? What if he's having sex with a woman in his room?

I stop in my tracks. I don't want to see that.

I'm standing there, beginning to attract attention, when a woman calls out, "Hey, there, Mona Wall. What's the hurry?"

And then a supermodel elbows me in the ribs and comes to a halt in front of me. She has an arm slung around a much younger man who could also come from a page in a magazine.

She's not dressed like anyone else in the place. She's wearing high-waisted, white palazzo pants, those expensive high-heeled shoes with the red bottoms, and a silky spaghetti strap top in silver that shows she's not wearing a bra, and even though she's a C-cup, she doesn't need one.

She reaches out her hand. "Harper Ruth. Heavy's sister."

Heavy is the MC president. I've heard about Harper. The old ladies do not speak kindly of her, and in the short time I've been back with John, I've heard her name a lot.

"Hey," the handsome kid with her protests.

"And Hobs' sister. Sorry. My bad." She tousles his hair, and he grins. Harper's older than me, maybe in her mid-thirties, and Hobs seems to be in his late teens. There's something off about him. He seems very...docile...for a kid his age.

"Hobs, can you go get us ladies two chardonnays?" Harper already has a full glass of red in her hand.

"I'm just here to see Wall," I finally manage to sputter.

"You know I'm just going to get lost." Hobs grins at his sister. He has the friendliest face.

"I know. But I thought it'd be rude to tell you to get lost." Harper swats him playfully on the butt, and he waves and ventures off. Harper throws her free arm over my shoulder.

Is she drunk?

Everything about her screams wasted, but her gray eyes are stone cold sober. I can see why the old ladies find her intimidating. There's also the fact she's a lawyer, and despite being a woman, she's involved in the club business. Deb, Pig Iron's wife, is involved, too. She's a bookkeeper or something. But Deb has a mom-vibe. Harper Ruth has a killer-clown-from-the-sewers vibe.

I want to go find John—I think—but she's latched on tight, and she's leading me to an overstuffed leather sofa in a far corner of the common room.

"Skeedaddle." She flicks her hand at the women who are squeezed bare thigh-to-thigh, five-wide on the sofa. Several blondes. None old enough to be Stephanie.

They cast us nasty looks as they tug down their skintight skirts and saunter off.

"It's good to be queen." Harper flashes me a frighteningly fake smile. "So." She flops down, dragging me with her. "Mona Wall. Are you a good witch or are you a bad witch?" She raises her perfectly sculpted eyebrows expectantly.

I don't have time for this.

But then again, am I in a hurry to find John in a back room with some woman? Maybe Harper's been sent to distract me while he sneaks a woman out the back. She is *very* distracting.

The smell of rum wafts past from a biker's glass. My stomach roils. I hate rum. First liquor I got drunk on. I clutch my stomach, and I flop forward, head between my knees, sucking down deep breaths and praying.

"Whoa! Prospect! Get a bucket!" Harper pulls my hair out of my face and scoots her fancy shoes as far away as she can.

"Where's the buckets?"

"Get a bucket substitute. You know what, dumbass. Give me that hat."

"I love this hat."

"I will kill and eat you."

And then there's a Pyle Tin Bangers baseball hat under

my face. I heave. Not much but spit and stomach acid. I feel better, though.

The hat disappears.

"What I do with this?"

"That you'll have to figure out for yourself. I'd recommend not putting it back on your head."

I lean back, recline my head on the back of the sofa, and I focus on breathing. Through my mouth. Not my nose.

Harper leans back beside me, turns her face to me, and downs almost a full glass of wine in one swallow. Her face is amazing. No visible makeup, but she has ruby red lips, and her eyelashes are super thick and long. Like a cartoon princess.

"I asked the wrong question. I should have asked if you'd like some water. Or crackers? What do pregnant ladies want?"

"Mercy," I moan.

She cackles. "And that's reason one thousand why I'm never having children. I've got Hobs. He's enough."

There's no way that boy is her biological child. She must see my confusion.

"My mom died when he was a baby. Breast cancer. I was thirteen. I raised him until I left for law school."

I hadn't heard this story.

"He's a cute kid."

"Thanks. I'd do anything for him."

I get that. The words agitate the terror pooling just under the surface of my skin. What if I'm losing this baby? How do I do this again?

Harper thwaps a hand on my thigh.

"What's that look for, Mrs. Wall?" Her face is inches from mine, her wine breath hot in my face. Weirdly, it doesn't make me want to puke.

I stare up at the exposed rafters of the clubhouse. "We lost three, uh, pregnancies. When John and I were together."

"Did they know why?"

"Nope. The doctor talked about the statistics the first time. And the second time, he said we were young. It wasn't time to worry yet. The third time he talked about going to a fertility doctor and doing some tests. But we never did that."

I don't know why I'm telling her this. I don't think I've ever talked about it with anyone. John knew. I didn't need to talk to him about it. He was there with me at every appointment, every step of the way. And my parents sure didn't want to hear about it.

Harper rests her forehead against mine. "Hobs has traumatic brain injury. I left for law school, and he got T.B.I. from a baseball bat. I was a shitty mother."

"I feel like that. I feel like I did something wrong, and I don't know what it was, so I can't stop doing it."

"It's the worst feeling in the world."

"Yeah."

"You didn't do anything wrong."

"Everyone says that."

"Doesn't make a difference."

"Not at all."

"I like you, Mona Wall. Even though your breath smells like puke."

"You're not as bad as they say you are, Harper Ruth."

She cracks up. "Yes, I am! Don't mess with my reputation, chickadee! I worked hard for it!"

"Is there mouthwash anywhere around here?"

"Yes. I'll take you to brush your teeth, and then I'll take you to your man. He's in the basement."

"You know where he is?" My gut swishes.

"He's where he always is. In the basement, lifting weights. Did you try to call him? He didn't answer?"

I nod.

"Yeah, reception is spotty down there."

I feel stupid. And relieved until I remember the spotting.

"Come on," Harper stands, grabbing my hand. "I'll show you to the bathroom the old ladies use. Much less likelihood that Creech is getting his knob polished in there."

"I'm an old lady?" Despite it all, the corners of my mouth creep up.

"Seems so."

Walking with Harper Ruth is like walking with a celebrity or a very dangerous animal. The women literally scurry out of her way. The men let her pass, but they follow her with their eyes. She's fearless. Totally unperturbed by it all. And it is *a lot*. The bathroom is by the back exit, and there's a fight going on in the yard, bare knuckles, and they're taking bets.

Most women I see now are topless. Even Deb. Good for her. She's got pretty perky boobs for a middle-aged woman.

If I knew what "wild" meant, John and I would have talked for a much, much longer time.

After the bathroom, Harper leads me to the stairs running to the basement of the modern annex. I avoided the toilet, and I've pulled myself together.

"You feeling better?" she asks.

"Minty fresh. Thank you."

"Go get your man."

"You sure he's down here?"

"He'll be down there. Once the tits come out, he disappears. He used to party, but after he patched in, he cleaned himself up. Never touches club pussy. Hasn't in years."

"He doesn't?" My heart warms.

"Nope." Harper gives me a strange, wistful smile. "Go straight at the bottom of the stairs. You won't be able to miss him. Man's aptly named." She winks and struts off, her perfect butt swaying as if she's moving to music.

I straighten my shoulders, and I venture down the stairs. I push open the double doors.

And there's John, standing in the middle of the mirrored room, shirtless, glistening with sweat. There are weight machines along one wall, free weights beside him.

And in front of him, there's a blond woman on her knees.

## 10

_____

### WALL


Something's wrong.

Mona's here; she comes through the door, and then her face loses all color. No. She's kind of green. She's gonna pass out.

I leap-trip over Cheyenne, who's doing some kind of stretch right in the middle of the free weight mat, trying to get Charge's attention.

Mona ducks, dodges past me, and shoves Cheyenne, sending her sprawling to the floor. What? Cheyenne pops up, and thank God Charge is there, because he snakes an arm around her mid-lunge before she can throw a punch.

Mona ain't never been in a fight before. She's got her fists balled up, thumbs inside for Chrissake, and she looks lost and mad as hell.

Cheyenne, on the other hand, is a scrapper like most of the sweetbutts. Mona ain't winnin' this one. I ease between them.

And then Mona lets one of those fists fly. Right into my face. The impact hardly registers; she has to reach so high she's got no force behind it. My jaw drops, more from surprise than anything else. She gasps and steps back, tripping over her own feet.

I scoop her up right when she sways, crumbles like a ragdoll, and bursts into loud, gushing tears. What the fuck is wrong?

"What's goin' on, baby?" She's cryin' so hard, she can't answer me. She rouses a little to slap at me and wriggle, but she's got no leverage.

"Wall?" Charge is at my side in a second, Forty close behind.

"Get some water."

Forty waves at Cheyenne to grab a bottle from the fridge. "I saw Sunny earlier. That means Larry's here."

"Mona don't need a dentist."

"He does other work, too."

"Okay. Somebody go get him." I don't know where to put Mona. There's nothing down here but equipment, so I sit on the lifting bench, keeping her in my arms. Besides, if I put her down, she might run. "Tell me what's wrong, baby." My stomach tightens. "Did that asshole bother you about his grandma's ring?"

We dumped Tommy at the county line, mouth nothing but bloody gums, and he swore we'd never see him again. It was kind of hard to understand him, though. Without the teeth.

Mona shakes her head, sobbing and straining against my arms.

I smooth her hair out of her face. She's wearing a shirt with weird bears on it. She must have come straight from work. Oh, shit. She probably called and got no answer. Reception down here sucks.

"Shit. Did you get worried when I didn't answer the

phone?" That can't be all of it. Mona cries a lot, but usually, it's 'cause she's mad.

She's glaring at Charge and Grinder, who've ambled over from the leg press, as if she's just noticing them.

"Back up. Give her some air."

Cheyenne's back with the water. She goes to hand it to Mona, and Mona stiffens, struggling to sit up. She still wants a piece of Cheyenne. I help her out, flip her so she's sitting upright in my lap, but I keep an arm around her waist.

"Stay away." She points at Cheyenne. "Stay the hell away from John, do you hear me?"

Cheyenne's brow furrows. Now that she's not in the moment, she's smart enough to tread carefully. "Okay." She eases back. "You want the water?"

Charge takes it from her and hands it to me. I unscrew the cap and press it into Mona's hand. "Drink."

She twists, craning her neck so she can see my face. Her nose is bright red and all scrunched up. "She wasn't giving you a blowjob?" She kind of belatedly looks down at my gym shorts.

Oh. That's what it looked like.

Shit. It's past midnight. Who knows what she walked through to get down here. Forty said it was getting wild when he came down. I figured I'd get one more set of reps in and head out. I didn't want to go back to an empty house.

Cheyenne raises her hands. "Hey. I don't mess with no one else's man."

"Girl, you been stretching in front of Charge the whole time I been down here." Grinder snorts. "And he's Harper's old man."

Cheyenne can't find anything to say to that. "I'm gonna go help Forty look for the dentist."

Mona's holding the water, not drinking. I tip it gently

from the bottom, and give my boys the eye. They follow Cheyenne upstairs. When the door swings shut behind them, the fight seeps out of my woman. She slumps. I rearrange her so she's sitting crossways on my lap. I need to see her face.

"I was working out. That's all, baby." If she don't believe me...Well, I guess I'll say it 'til she does.

She reaches out and runs soft fingers along my jaw. "I hit you."

"It didn't hurt none."

Her lips turn down, and she flexes her hand. "It hurt my hand."

I grab it and kiss the knuckles. When Forty gets back, he's gonna need to go for some ice.

"I'm sorry my face hurt your hand."

She gives me a tiny smile. She still looks like hell. Pale, green, and her skin's cold to the touch.

"What happened, baby? Were you freaked out when you couldn't get me on the phone?"

"No." The tears come in another flood.

I used to hate a woman crying, but being married to Mona, I got used to them. She's just a weeper. She ain't weak, it's just what she needs to get her mouth goin'.

"Yes," she manages to get out between sobs. "You always pick up. Why didn't you tell me you wouldn't have service? I was speeding, and I slid, and then I fell in the snow, and I threw up in a man's hat."

There it is. It's all coming out. And what the fuck? That tin piece of shit is getting traded in for something with four-wheel drive tomorrow.

"Whose hat did you puke in?" Who was close enough to her in this condition and didn't come get me immediately?

"Some kid. Prospect?"

That don't narrow it down much. We got a bumper crop right now.

And then she kind of gags. Her throat works, and she mashes her lips together and closes her eyes. Oh, shit. She's knocked up.

I stand, hoist her to my side, and haul her ass to the trashcan.

"Oh, John, no! The smell! No!"

Oh, yeah. What else is there? The towel hamper? I've got her halfway there when that smell hits me.

"Just put me down." She's slapping at me weakly. "Put me down, and I'll be fine. But not by that hamper."

I return her to the bench, but this time, I kneel on the mat, so we're eye to eye. And there's some distance in case she hurls. She wasn't sick much with Peanut and Jellybean, but she was a champion puker with Lemon. One of the reasons we thought she was gonna be okay.

I let the sadness swell for a little, and then I tuck it back. Took me a long time to learn how to do that. Heavy helped. And working outside with my hands, not living emergency to emergency.

And I don't have a clue what road Mona's come down with the losses. We haven't talked about it. We never did.

And that was the problem, wasn't it? I tried to fix it with flowers and day trips and bike rides and date nights, and she didn't want none of that. Flowers in the trash 'cause they smelled like a funeral, she said. Lake Patonquin had too many mosquitos, Pyle had too many people, and there was no movie she wanted to see.

There was nothin' I could do to make her happy but leave her alone.

And she got sadder and sadder.

And I got—weak. I got weak, and I fucked up, and we

didn't talk about it then, neither. She said leave. I left. 'Cause there was nothing I could do, was there?

Except I could have talked. I could have made her listen.

Any time after I pulled myself together, I could have picked up the phone. But I let shame get between us. It's easier to be a wrong man than a weak man, right?

Easier to say nothing than try to fix things and make it worse with your words. The neckline of Mona's scrubs is wet from her tears. I don't think words could make shit worse at this point.

I exhale a long breath. This is not my fuckin' forte.

"You're pregnant."

She inhales on a sob, wrapping her arm around her lower belly. "I don't know. I'm spotting. I took a test. It was positive, but I'm spotting."

Oh, fuck. I sit back on my heels, and she stands, really to bolt. I grab her calves.

"Sit back down, Mona. Talk to me."

She looks down, and I look up, a man on his knees, praying, trying to pin the whole world with his eyes.

"Sit down, Mona. Please."

"I can't do this again."

"I'm here, baby. You ain't alone."

"You *left*." Her voice breaks.

"No. I, mean, I did. I left that night, and I—I went on a binge until I hit rock bottom. But when I got my head straight, you need to know, I came back. And I was always there."

Her face is hardening. She don't believe me.

"Do you know how many nights I slept in my truck in front of the Chaudharys? They called the cops. I had to talk to Ajay. Explain that sometimes I can't sleep unless I know you're okay." Most embarrassing conversation of my life.

"I drove by Shady Acres. I'd follow you home sometimes at the end of your shift. I take Greg out for beers all the time just so he'll talk about Lorraine and maybe mention you. I fuckin' hate that guy."

Mona's staring at the floor, chewing that lower lip. What's goin' on in her head?

"I ain't been with you, Mona, but I been around. I couldn't leave you. You're my world."

Then her eyes meet mine, and there's so much fear there.

"What if it happens again? What if I can't handle it, and I push you away, and I lose you again? What if I can't have babies, and it tears us apart?"

Shit. Yeah. The same questions have been keeping me up at night. I turn on the bedside lamp once she falls asleep so I can watch her, memorize her beautiful face, store up enough of her to keep me alive if it all goes south again. Even though, I know I couldn't bear losin' her twice.

My hands tighter and slide down to her ankles. Her socks are cold and wet. I hold on, try to warm her up.

"You remember the fire out on Hammerbacher Road?"

"The one with the barn where the horses got loose?"

"No. That was on Old Bachman Road. The one on Hammerbacher was a couple weeks after—after we lost Lemon. An elderly couple. She had dementia. Early stages. He was at a bull roast at the Elk Lodge. He came home; the place was in flames. He called us, and then he went in for her. We found them both on the stairs. He'd got her that far."

She slides down to the floor. There's not much room between me and the bench, so she's kneeling between my knees. She grabs my hands, holds them tight with all her strength.

"I don't remember that."

"It was in the news. You might not have seen it." She was real out of it then. She'd stare at the television, but she wasn't really watching.

"You worked that fire?"

"Yeah. I found them. He'd wrapped a pillow case around her face as a mask."

"Oh, John." She squeezes my hands even tighter.

"That happened, right after we lost Lemon. And I got up, showered, went to work. And I tried to get you to come places with me. Or eat. I made you that appointment with the hair dresser, and you cried, and I felt like a total asshole—"

She don't look too good, so I wrap my big ol' arms around her to keep her steady.

"I tried to fix it, and I couldn't, and it killed me. And shit could very well go wrong again, and I won't be able to fix it."

I worked so hard these past four years to be bigger, stronger, super-fuckin'-human. But the truth has a way of starin' you in the face. Some shit cannot be beat into submission.

I'm looking past her, at the clock. Not 'cause I care about the time, but 'cause I can't bear to see her disappointment. I can't watch her give up on me again.

She rests her forehead on my chest.

"I left you," she says. "I didn't even know how far gone I was until I wasn't anymore."

"You went through hell."

"It was months before I got myself together enough to get a haircut."

"I know. That was a good day."

"You saw my haircut?" She swipes her face on my shirt,

sniffles, and looks up. There's my beautiful wife. Still here. In my arms.

"I was working construction by then. I'd drive by the nursing home on my lunch hour. Check on you. I didn't see your car. Kind of panicked. Drove around town. Lucked out seeing you come out of the barbershop."

"Hair salon."

"You were smiling, and you kept touching your hair." I stroke a lock between my fingers. It's a miracle to me how soft it always is.

"I'd signed up for nursing classes."

"I was so proud of you. I *am* so proud of you."

She blushes a little. Ducks her head. And then her face falls. "What if I'm losing this baby?"

"Is it bad yet?"

She shakes her head. "Only spotting."

"We'll go to the doctor tomorrow. Steel Bones has an in. We won't need to wait for an appointment."

We both know at this stage, there ain't much a doctor can do, but she relaxes a little in my arms.

She sighs. "We're being reckless, aren't we? Shacking up so quickly and having a baby after everything we've been through."

I gesture toward the ceiling. A bass beat and stomping feet are seeping through. "I'm in a biker gang. I ain't worried about reckless."

"My mother would tell me I'm being stupid."

"My mother'll hug you 'til you squeal and feed you 'til you can't stand." That got a smile out of her. Quick, but it counts.

Then, she's quiet a long time. I rest my hands on her hips and wait.

"John, what if we can't ever have a baby?"

That's the question, ain't it? And I ain't got an answer.

"Baby, can I take you for a ride?"

She knits her brow. "It's thirty degrees out there."

"Not on my bike. In my truck."

"Now?"

"Yeah." It's a little past two in the morning, but where I want to go doesn't close.

"Um. Okay?" She glances down at herself.

First, we got to get her into something warmer and drier. I stand, and hold out my hand, palm up.

"Trust me?"

She don't take a second to slide her small fingers in mine. My heart fills to bursting.

# 11

## MONA

John leads me up two flights of stairs to his room. I imagined a cramped dorm room, I guess, but his place is in the clubhouse's modern annex. It's like an apartment, a nice one. He has a kitchenette, a bathroom, hardwood floors, recessed lighting, the works.

It's pretty bare. Furniture, free weights, a chin up bar in the bathroom doorway. And our wedding picture. Not the big one, but a small one, sitting on his bedside table. I flop down on the bed and pick it up. It's two-sided. Me and him, standing awkwardly side-by-side, like the farm couple in that painting. Neither of us are photogenic.

The other picture is when the photographer lined up all the Walls. They're a huge family, in number and size, so he had to take the shot from far back. There's John Senior and Mama Kelly, John and I, and then Kellum, Cashel, Dina, and Jesse. Dina and I are so short in comparison, we look like kids.

John Senior is serious as the pope. Each of the boys are wearing a different, doofy expression. Dina's wearing her usual thousand-yard stare. Mama Kelly and I are cracking up.

My hand creeps to my belly.

I want this. So bad. My heart thuds in my chest. The urge to lay down, stay stock-still, and pray overwhelms me.

"Put this on." John hands me a pair of his gym socks and sweat pants.

"I'm going to look ridiculous in those pants."

"No one will see but me." Before I can move, he yanks off my shoes and peels off a sock.

"Hey!" It's been a long day. I nudge him off. He doesn't need to be near my feet. I change quickly. Good thing the sweatpants have a drawstring. I have to roll them up at the ankles, and it still looks like I'm wearing a huge, black sack.

"Ready?" He's got his keys, and he's holding out a brown, fur-lined jacket.

"Where are we going?"

"Little tour. Don't worry. We ain't gonna run into anyone."

I have no clue what he's up to, but I'm beyond emotionally drained, way too wired to sleep, and all I want to do is go along with John.

Sometime in the past half hour or so, he became yet another man to me. Or I became another me?

Anyway, I go along as he leads me to his truck, helps me up, and buckles me in. He digs a pair of leather mittens out of the glove box. They smell like pine sap.

"Put these on until the cab warms up."

He turns the key, and we sit in silence as he lets the engine warm up. The sky has cleared, and there's a smattering of stars, far away, but still pretty. Eventually, we can't see our breath anymore, and John pulls off toward town.

"We're going to Petty's Mill?" I guess I figured he was driving us home.

"Yup."

Petty's Mill is an older town than Shady Gap. Shady Gap has the county's big box stores and the community college, but Petty's Mill has the historic downtown and riverfront development.

That seems to be where we're heading. John drives the speed limit past rehabbed Victorians and brand-new boutiques. There are still rough looking streets, but the closer you get to the river, the more you see that money is being invested in this town.

John parks in a public lot at the Promenade. The Promenade is all new. There are restaurants where the lettuce is "locally sourced," so the sandwiches cost double. A bunch of stores that sell candles and watercolors of waterfowl.

I wait for him; he helps me down. His truck's a good foot and a half off the ground, and it's icy. There's a bitter wind coming off the river. The stars are nice, but the cold is brutal. My teeth start chattering.

"It ain't too far. I'll get you warmed back up real soon."

He leads me to a dock built for people strolling the Promenade. There are benches and fancy streetlights made to look like gas lamps. It's paved with bricks, the kind you can buy and have inscribed with your name.

John's scanning the ground, looking for something. "Here," he says. He points down.

There's a brick that reads *Peanut, Jellybean, and Lemon.*

"I bought that for a thousand bucks at auction."

He searches my face. He's drawn himself up, bracing for my reaction. The wind ruffles his hair, and it strikes me again how crazy it is that this enormous man can be so intent on plain ol' me.

I glance down at the brick.

It hurts, but also...it's good. There should be a marker. There should be a place.

"My dad used to bring us down here to fish. Before they renovated the waterfront. There used to be a concrete dock here. In the summer, the ice cream truck would come by. The old guys would cuss out the ice cream man for scaring off the fish. Us kids loved it."

I should have thought of doing something like this. Guilt shoots straight through my chest, an arrow with jagged edges.

"What is that baby? What's that look?"

"I don't know." I jam my gloved hands into my pockets. "I've never—I—never mind."

"You can tell me. Anything. I can take it, baby. I can carry anything for you."

My eyes burn, but there are no tears left. I take my hand out of my pocket, wind my arm through John's, and tuck it back in.

"I just feel so guilty sometimes. Like I did something wrong, and I'm such an emotional coward that all I did was put everything in a box in the garage. Maybe I would have a made a shitty mother. Maybe that's why it played out the way it did."

"You're gonna be a great mother."

"How do you know?"

He shrugs. "I got a great one. Know one when I see one, I guess." It's not a platitude. He's being serious.

He does have a great mom. Kelly Wall is a force of nature, almost six feet tall herself and always laughing.

"You don't believe me?"

I shake my head.

"Like the shirt says, no worries. I'll help you out. I'm

gonna be an awesome dad."

"How can you be so confident?"

John shrugs. "I got the love in my heart, you know? I figure if I stay of sound body, the rest will follow."

"As simple as that?"

"Loving and caring for kids never looked hard in my house comin' up."

I flush. Another thing John and I don't talk about. The fact that once I turned eighteen and moved out, if I didn't call my parents, I don't think I'd ever hear from them.

"I want to do everything different from my parents."

"Okay." John sets his chin on top of my head. A car whooshes by in the slush. After a long minute, John asks, "Ready?"

He takes my elbow and he leads me back to the truck. I figure we're going home now, but instead we head south, towards where his parents live.

"You too tired, or can I show you one more thing?"

"I'm not tired."

"It's late. You can rest on the way. It's about a forty-minute drive."

As we drive, the cab grows warm and cozy. I lean my head on the cool glass of the window, and watch the countryside. The night's grayish now, not pitch black. The stars have faded away. John turns the radio to the country station.

My eyelids drift shut, and I'm not exactly asleep, I'm sort of floating, cozy in the fur-lined coat and thick, wool socks. I feel safe. I feel like I'm exactly where I'm supposed to be.

I rouse to the crank of John engaging the emergency brake. We're way out in the country now. Dawn has broken, casting a weak light over snowy fields and distant woods. I recognize where we are in an instant. The Wade Arboretum outside of Pyle. John brought me here on one of our first dates.

"Here. We got to walk a little ways, and the paths ain't shoveled." John has opened the passenger side door, letting a gust of cold air in, and he's holding up a pair of his construction boots.

"I can't wear those. I'll fall out of them."

"I'll carry you then."

"That's ridiculous." I eye the boots. "I'll tie them tight." Of course, John helps me get them on, and lifts me down from the truck. They're like clown shoes. I have to lift my feet super high with each step.

"Is it far?"

"Not very."

The sun's all the way up before we get where we're going, though. We're standing in front of a fairly small, leafless tree, shrouded in snow. There are two other trees like it a yard or so away, much bigger, with cool, gnarled trunks.

"That's a bur oak. It'll get anywhere from fifty to eighty feet tall."

It's so small.

"That's our babies' tree?"

"That's their tree." John wraps his arms around me. The wind gusts, and snow crystals sting my cheeks. I sniff. My nose is running from the cold.

It's lonely out here now, but I've been here in the summer. John brought me on one of our early dates. Our first long bike ride together. My thighs ached afterwards for days. It was gorgeous that day. A bright blue sky. No humidity. All the leaves rustling, and the birds so busy, sailing overhead from tree to tree.

A perfect day.

"How long ago did you have it planted?"

"Come this spring, it'll be two years."

"It's doing okay so far?"

"It's grown a good bit. It's holding its own."

We're quiet a long time.

"I'm scared, John."

"Me, too, babe."

I lean back into him, let his strength take my weight.

"It's a good tree," I say.

John drops a kiss on the top of my head. "We'll come back in spring. It's got great leaves."

"You picked a good one."

"I know I did." He draws me closer. "I'd pick you again. Every time."

I look up at his dark brown eyes. He tightens his grip around my waist. I tilt up my head. He takes my mouth, hungry and warm and sweet as home.

"Can I take you home, Mrs. Wall?" he asks between kisses.

"Yes, please, Mr. Wall," I reply.

# EPILOGUE
## WALL

**P**itocin is a son of a bitch.

At the class the hospital makes you take, they have you put your fingers in a cup of ice and hold them there. And that's supposed to be like the pain of contractions. And then you take your fingers out and warm 'em up, and a minute or whatever later, you stick 'em back in.

But Pitocin contractions are different. They're comin' so close together, Mona don't have a chance to catch her breath. It ain't no frozen fingers, either. She's pasty white, sweating bullets, and I don't like the way the machines are beeping.

My girl was tryin' to do it without meds—somehow her mother got in her ear about epidurals bein' for pussies or something—and now that the pain's too bad, she's agreed to do meds, but they got to hydrate her before they can do the spinal tap.

This is bullshit. She's hurtin' so bad for no reason. And she don't look good.

"How you doin', baby?"

She can't really talk no more; she's mostly hyperventi-lating and grittin' her teeth, but I can't help but ask.

Mona grunts.

"You're doin' great."

I know I said I wanted a big family like the one I come from, but I have changed my mind. The past eight-and-a-half months have been hell. First, there was the implanta-tion bleeding. We got through that. Then they thought she had hyperemesis gravidarum she was puking so much, and that led to the iron deficiency.

Then they found out the baby has a single umbilical artery, which isn't a big deal, except it is. That's why the baby has to get popped early with the Pitocin.

And this is the weird part—Mona's been cool as a cucumber after that first panic. She gets upset; she drives out to our tree. Or I drive her. Since she got the big belly, I don't like her drivin'.

She ain't cried once. It's like she's becoming one of those mama bears. She'll cuss you out now. It's cute as hell.

"Mr. Wall?"

A nurse tries to scoot past me. This room's too small, but I ain't leaving, so I suck in what I can to let her through.

"Is this normal?" I gesture to the machine behind Mona's bed. I ask all of the nurses. Most foist me off on someone else, tell me the doctor will talk to me when she comes by, but I ain't seen hide nor hair of her since two hours ago. Mona was still holdin' my hand, then. Now she's got her fists balled close by her sides.

The nurse squints at the monitor. "Looks good. How you feelin'?" She brushes damp hair from Mona's forehead. The lady's my mom's age, short gray hair, glasses on a string around her neck.

Mona looks to me, so I answer for her. "She don't feel good. How much longer 'til she can get the epidural?"

The nurse watches the black lines go up and down a few seconds longer. "I'm going to call Dr. Ephron. I don't think there's going to be time for the epidural."

Mona lets out an awful sound, half sob, half scream. My muscles tense all over my body.

I'm scared as hell. My body wants to fight, and I'm surrounded by women, a thing called a panda warmer, and a white board that says *Goal: Meet Baby Wall.*

I screw my eyes shut, 'cause that's all I can do, and then a small, clammy hand slips into mine.

"How you doing, John?" Mona pants through clenched teeth.

Hot damn, she's beautiful. Her hair's stickin' to her head, and her pupils are blown out. Her boobs are massive, hanging out of the hospital gown that's all askew. And her belly. It's huge with angry red lines all over like someone cracked an egg.

That's my baby in there.

"I'm great, Mona. Hang on." Her belly kind of quivers, and a foot bulges by her rib. I reach out and rest my hand on the little kicker. This kid is strong as hell. He's been whoopin' up on her insides for months now.

We found out about the single umbilical artery at the twenty-week ultrasound. Just when Mona was starting to sleep a little better. Wham. We had a hard, few days. We talked through it. Well, Mona lost her shit, I dragged her to bed, and made her cum until she started babbling like she does when she's dicked out of her mind.

"You decided on a name yet?" the nurse asks.

Mona's hand tightens on mine, a low moan interrupting her response.

"I'm letting her pick," I answer for her.

It takes Mona a half-minute to catch her breath and pant, "I already picked."

"You said Margaret or Ansley for a girl, and John or Wyatt for a boy. You didn't pick which."

Another nurse and young guy in a white coat who introduced himself as the intern or something filter in. The nurse is pushing a cart filled with stuff. I guess shit is about to go down. My heart starts beating against my ribs. This is it.

"I want you to pick, babe," I tell her, hunkering down. "I like 'em all."

"You—" She's huffin' and puffin'. "Pick!"

"Baby, it's all you." I bend over, press my forehead to her sweaty brow. "You're about to give me everything I ever wanted. I want you to have it your way."

"Awww."

I look up. About six people in scrubs are standing at the foot of Mona's bed. Her knees are up, and her robe's undone. She's buck ass naked, and I don't think she's even noticed. She's got her eyes locked on mine.

"Can I get you to hold her leg?" the doc asks me, and then she shows me how to cradle Mona's thigh while she coaches her to push and bear down, and there is a shit ton of blood, and I ain't never been so scared in my entire life.

And then a baby cries.

"It's a girl!" Doctor Ephron snaps off her gloves, and a nurse already has this super tiny, squalling, red thing. They mess with her, and then they bring her—my daughter—to Mona and lay her on her bare chest. I hunch down, get eye level. The instant she touches Mona's skin, she calms. Falls straight asleep.

"Am I supposed to get her to nurse?" Mona's eyes are fading. She's exhausted. I stroke her damp hair.

"Rest your eyes a second, Mona."

The doctors are still doin' something between her legs, but the room feels still. It's eleven nineteen in the morning. And I have a daughter.

"John," Mona murmurs, on the verge of passing out.

"Yes, baby."

"Her name is Hope."

"Hope?"

"Yeah." She's drifting off. My daughter—Hope—is already asleep, nuzzled to her chest. I stand over them, awed and proud and praising God.

There are miracles in this wicked world still.

I should know. I'm lookin' at two of them.

THE STEEL BONES Motorcycle Club saga continues in Forty!

## A NOTE FROM THE AUTHOR

Will Ernestine ever take Grinder back?
Will Creech ever find someone who can love him?
Who was Boots' "California Girl' and why did she leave?

I have no idea! But you will be the first to know if you sign up for my newsletter at www.catecwells.com.

You'll get a FREE novella, too!

## ABOUT THE AUTHOR

Cate C. Wells indulges herself in everything from motorcycle club to small town to mafia to paranormal romance. Whatever the subgenera, readers can expect character-driven stories that are raw, real, and emotionally satisfying. She's into messy love, flaws, long roads to redemption, grace, and happily ever after, in books and in life.

Along with stories, she's collected a husband and three children along the way. She lives in Baltimore when she's not exploring the world with the family.

I love to connect with readers! Meet me in The Cate C. Wells Reader Group on Facebook.

Facebook: @catecwells
Twitter: @CateCWells1
Bookbub: @catecwells

Printed in Great Britain
by Amazon

21532401R00098